THE BANDIT OF MOK HILL

THE BANDIT
of MOK HILL

. . . .

by Evelyn Sibley Lampman

Illustrated by Marvin Friedman

Doubleday & Company, Inc., Garden City, New York

*For Adam Bronson McIsaac
with love from Gam*

Chapter 1

Angel's thin hand closed around the neck of the heavy glass bottle beside him, and he flung it expertly in the direction of the small sound that had roused him from sleep. There was a deadened thud as the missile found its mark, followed by a high "eek" of pain and terror, and in the darkness Angel smiled with satisfaction.

"Accursed rat," he said in Spanish.

"What is it? Is it the Catcher?" Pierre's frightened voice came from across the cabin, and there was the rustling of straw as he sat up in the bunk. Awakened from a sound sleep, his words had been in his mother tongue, but even if Angel had not recognized the French for "catcher" he would have known the reason for his friend's terror. It was all they thought about these days.

"No, just another rat," he explained kindly and in English. "This ship's crawling with them. They're worse than lice. I had ten bottles lined up beside me last night, and I just threw the last one. We won't sleep here again."

"Certainly not," said Pierre fearfully. "You know our rule."

"I ought to," agreed Angel with pride. "I thought of it. And it's kept us safe from the Catcher, too."

The rule was very simple, although sometimes it was a nuisance. When they were already tired it was a temptation to find sleeping space in one of the closer ships, and not to go jumping and swinging from bark to brig to schooner to sloop, just because the rule was never to sleep twice in the same place.

Their choices seemed inexhaustible, for there were over five hundred vessels moored side by side and end to end in Yerba Buena Cove, and another hundred big square-riggers elsewhere in the bay and river. They had one thing in common, these silent, weathering ships with bare riggings: their officers and crews had all deserted for the gold mines. Some had been there as long as three and a half years, and everything of value that could be carried away had already been taken. A few had been dragged out of the water and converted into gambling palaces or warehouses, for new lumber was expensive in the booming San Francisco of 1851, and the councilmen were grumbling that action must be taken soon about the remaining vessels. Why, there were almost more ships in the harbor than houses in the city, and they were an open invitation to the lawless! Criminals used them as hiding places, and homeless men slept on their decks, thereby cheating good honest innkeepers the price of a night's lodging.

Neither the criminals nor the vagrants bothered Angel or Pierre. When the boys discovered that a ship was occupied, they merely jumped over railings until they found an empty one. They were never challenged. There was nothing about the sight of two ragged twelve-year-olds to alarm those already in possession. San Francisco was filled with deserted waifs and orphans—or it had been until lately when, in desperation, the council had established an orphan asylum and begun rounding them up.

"It is morning." Pierre's voice sounded doubtful, and the straw rustled again in the darkness.

"Foggy, too," agreed Angel. He could feel damp wisps coming through the broken glass above his head. Fog acted like a curtain, shutting out much of the early dawn, but he did not need light to tell him it was another day. His empty stomach was proof enough.

There were two sharp, important whacks as Pierre's new boots struck the wooden floor. Hearing them, Angel tried to put down a little stab of jealousy. He wished he had been there instead of Pierre when the trader set out the heavy boots and then foolishly turned his back. Then he remembered the teachings of the old priest at Valparaiso. Envy was a sin. He must rejoice in his friend's good fortune at having secured a new pair of boots that almost fit.

The air was moist and cold when they came on deck, and the fog was so thick they could not see the ships closely moored on either side of their own.

"A good day." Angel's voice was pleased. "The Catcher won't come out in this. He couldn't see past his own nose."

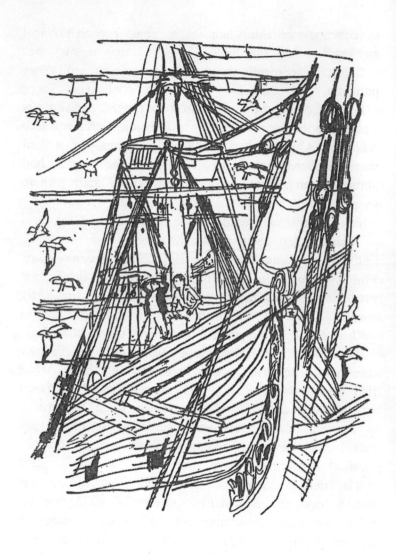

"Maybe he'll give up pretty soon, anyway," said Pierre hopefully. "He's got most of us. All the little ones. They went first because they didn't care. Some of them were even glad about it. I don't know why they want to put the old ones like us in their orphan asylum, anyway."

"To take care of the little ones," explained Angel patiently.

For a moment he remembered those long ago days in Valparaiso before Mamacita had married Mr. Schmidt. Although Angel had no brothers or sisters of his own, there had been dozens of cousins living in the cave house above the city. The big ones were always given the responsibility of looking after the little ones. How could a family manage otherwise?

"The Catcher won't give up," he added positively. "Not until he has every one of us in his new orphan asylum. The big ones especially. Ned and Rosie and Jigger and you and me and all the rest. He needs us to do the work."

"I won't work for them," declared Pierre. "I refuse."

"You'll work if they catch you." Angel pulled his thin coat a little closer about his shivering body. "And they'll catch us sooner or later if we stay here. That's why we have to leave."

"Leave? Where would we go?" Pierre's tone suggested that there was no other place in the world.

"To the diggings first."

"To the gold mines? You think perhaps we will find a fortune?" At first Pierre was intrigued, but the next moment he was doubtful. "They say everyone is not lucky, Angel. They say that digging gold is hard. Maybe even harder than working in the orphan asylum."

"We aren't going to dig," Angel told him irritably. "We're going to find my friend. My good friend Joaquin Murieta. We are going to be bandits, Pierre!"

5

"Bandits?" This time there was definite protest in Pierre's voice. "But bandits are hunted. They are shot. And they shoot others. I do not think I could shoot anybody, Angel."

"We'll talk about it later," said Angel soothingly. He had already made up his mind, and he hoped he could talk Pierre into the plan. Angel didn't want to be all alone again. It was too frightening. "Let's get something to eat. It will be easy today with the fog so thick."

It took some time to make their way to shore for each night they were having to go farther and farther out to find a bedroom they had not used before. Full daylight had arrived by the time Pierre's new boots and Angel's worn ones touched the damp, gritty wharf, but their friend the fog still swirled about them.

"Breakfast first," said Pierre eagerly. "Come along."

He led the way unerringly toward one of the rough-planked streets that led up from the bay. On either side the boards were laid at an angle, forming a sidewalk before rows of small shops. Some of these were still in the process of construction, but others were shedlike affairs built of wood, while a few of the older ones were made of canvas. All were open on the side next to the street. The fog-shrouded hulks of their proprietors lurked within, sometimes moving to the front at the sound of footsteps; if the steps continued on, they returned to the shop's interior.

It was necessary to go single file, for the narrow walkway was partially blocked by barrels and crates, boxes, and sacks of goods awaiting storage space in the already cramped interiors. An effort had been made to nail everything shut for the night, but both Angel and

Pierre had small hands and deft fingers. Although they had not seemed to linger at any time, their pockets were bulging by the time they reached the last of the markets.

"What did you get?" asked Pierre eagerly.

"Let's go up Pacific Street and sit down," said Angel, ignoring the question. "The Catcher won't come there, and if he does he'll think we're just a couple more Mexicans and belong to somebody."

"I do not look like a Mexican," objected Pierre indignantly. "I am French." But he followed along willingly.

Although Angel felt safe in the little Mexican quarter along Pacific Street, it always made him feel sad. The first time he had been there was that terrible night three years ago when the Hounds ran wild. He and Mamacita had been in San Francisco less than a week when it happened.

Mamacita had married Mr. Schmidt, who was a very important man, the third mate on a sailing ship that put in at Valparaiso for repairs. In spite of his importance, Angel hadn't liked him even then, and couldn't see why Mamacita had wished to marry him and leave Valparaiso and all their family and friends. But she did. She was as stubborn as she was pretty. Even Mr. Schmidt couldn't change her mind once she made it up. Mr. Schmidt hadn't wanted her to bring Angel, her only son, the comfort of her life since the death of her dear first husband. But Mamacita wouldn't marry Mr. Schmidt and sail away without Angel, not for all the California gold she could gather in her apron. So Mr. Schmidt had had to give in, since he wanted to marry Mamacita, and the three of them had come by bark to San Francisco.

For four days they stayed in a boardinghouse, and it was very lonely for no one there spoke Spanish except Mr. Schmidt, who was always out seeing to things, and Mamacita and Angel did not understand English. The two of them took short walks each evening, being careful to stay within eye distance of the boardinghouse so they would not get lost.

On one of these excursions they met a man who looked so much like the people of Valparaiso that Mamacita, on an impulse, said *"Buenas tardes,"* and the man stopped and answered her politely in the same tongue.

To their delight they learned that like themselves he was Chilean, from Santiago no less, and it was like greeting an old friend. There was a whole colony of their countrymen in San Francisco, he told them—gentlemen, ladies, and children too—and at that very moment he was on his way to join them. If the señora and her son wished to accompany him and visit for a few moments with those from home, he would escort them back to the boardinghouse afterward.

Mamacita had not hesitated. She had been lonely, and the man was obviously a gentleman. She took Angel's hand firmly, and they started walking up one of the many steep hills on which this strange city had been built. Before long they encountered the group of Chileans promenading in the warm twilight. They welcomed Mamacita and Angel as friends and, as they walked together, they exchanged reminiscences of home and their impressions of this alien land.

Suddenly, and without warning, there was a great commotion behind them. Angry male voices shouted words that Angel could not understand. The little group of promenaders stopped, startled. A crowd of men wearing masks over their faces and carrying lighted torches was running toward them.

"The Hounds!" cried one of the Chileans, stepping quickly in front of his wife.

Clutching their children, the other Chilean women gathered in a tight knot behind their men. They had been in San Francisco long enough to have heard stories about the Hounds, a group of ruffians who made their own laws and had sworn to rid the city of anyone whose skin was a shade darker than their own. The Mexicans and the Chinese had been the favorite targets of the Hounds, and at the moment they were on their way to burn the tents of the Mexicans on Telegraph Hill. This little group of unprotected Chileans was an unexpected diversion. It was almost as though they were offering themselves as a sacrifice.

Mamacita did not know about the Hounds, but she recognized the threat in the rough, angry voices. In an instant she saw the flash of steel knives and the metallic sheen of gun barrels under the torches. She pushed Angel away from her, heading him toward the darkness of the hill.

"Run!" she ordered. "Run as you have never run before."

Angel had not wanted to leave her.

"Mamacita—"

"Run!" When she used that tone there was to be no further argument. "Run!"

Angel ran. Through the darkness, up the rough road that was little more than a trail ascending the hill, he ran as fast as his nine-year-old legs could carry him.

Sometimes a foot sank in a pothole and he fell to his knees, but the next moment he was up and hurrying on. Behind him he could hear the sounds, the terrible sounds that would stay with him all his life—men shouting, women and children screaming, the explosion of guns. Mamacita was there, in the midst of all that horror! Part of him wanted to go back and defend her, but another part hurried him on.

At last he reached the small Mexican quarter. Their tents were all around him. There had been lights within, but as the sounds of conflict floated up the hill, candles had been blown out, leaving the tents like a gathering of pale ghosts in the twilight.

Tears were running down Angel's face and his breath was coming in aching gasps, each one a little more painful than the one before. He faltered, wondering whether the occupants of these tents were friends or were like the masked men at the foot of the hill. Before he could make up his mind, the flap of one of them was pushed open and a young Mexican stepped outside.

For a moment they stood there staring at each other, the slim, olive-skinned stranger and the frightened, panting boy. Then the Mexican smiled and held out his hand.

"You have escaped them," he said in Spanish. "That is good. Come inside. My home is your home. You will be safe. They will have had enough of bloodletting for one night."

The young man had spoken the truth. The Hounds had been satisfied with the massacre of the Chileans and had not continued up the hill. But Angel never saw Mamacita again, and whenever he returned to this place the memory made him unhappy.

Pierre, to whom Angel had never confided the story, had no such feelings. He was happy as they climbed the hill. They found a smooth place to sit down, with a huge boulder as a back rest, and immediately began unloading their pockets.

"An apple from the north," enumerated Pierre, starting a pile of stolen loot on the ground beside him. "And an orange from the south. From Chile, perhaps, Angel? A handful of sugar from some hot island—"

"You'd better leave that in your pocket," advised Angel hastily. "Unless you want to eat it right away."

"A good idea," approved Pierre, stuffing his mouth with loose sugar and licking his fingers. "I got some sailor's biscuits. Harder than rocks. We need water to soak them in."

"Jake Plumber, the band leader, says it's the spring water here that makes people sick," said Angel, inspecting a potato and wondering whether to eat it raw or save it for roasting at some time when they had a fire. "He says at least ten men die every day from drinking the water here."

"I don't like water anyway," said Pierre. "At home nobody drinks water. But you drink it sometimes, Angel. It never made you sick."

"Maybe it's because I didn't know about it," decided Angel. "Now that Jake told me, I'll have to be careful. If you know that something might make you sick, it's sure to. And I can't get sick just when I'm going to be a bandit," he added craftily.

"How do you know Joaquin Murieta will take you?" Pierre frowned. "Bandits need men. Why would he bother with a boy?"

11

"Because that's the kind of a man he is. And besides he isn't so very old himself."

"Tell me about him again," ordered Pierre, chewing thoughtfully.

"It was night," began Angel promptly. This part of the story, the encounter with the celebrated Joaquin Murieta, he did not mind discussing. It was only the part about Mamacita that was too personal for outsiders. "I was running away from the Hounds. It was their last night. The night before the Vigilantes organized and ran them out of town."

"Skip that part," said Pierre impatiently. "Start with Joaquin."

"I was running away from the Hounds," insisted Angel stubbornly, "and I got to the Mexican tents. I was tired. I couldn't run any more. Then Joaquin stepped out of his tent, only, of course, I didn't know who he was. Nobody did. He wasn't famous then. He and Rosita had only just come to San Francisco. He told me to come inside, and I did."

"What did he look like?" demanded Pierre.

"He was handsome. Not so tall as some Americans grow, but tall for a Mexican. He had brown eyes and black hair, which fell to here." Angel indicated his shoulders. "He moved quickly, and his fingers were long and thin. I remember that he kept moving them, first one hand and then the other, like a drummer who beats time with a band."

"And he was kind to you?"

"Yes. So was Rosita. We just sat there in the dark, all of us. Listening." Angel shuddered in spite of his efforts not to. "Listening to the Hounds at the bottom

12

of the hill. Even after they were gone, we just sat there. Rosita had her arm around me, and Joaquin leaned over and patted my knee. He said, 'Someday, little one, I will avenge this night and all the other nights like it. I swear it. Men will hear of me. Of Joaquin, the avenger.' And he meant it."

"But he only said Joaquin," insisted Pierre. "He did not say Joaquin Murieta."

"No." Angel made the admission reluctantly. "But would there be two Joaquins who are bandits? They say that after a raid, or when someone has been stripped of his gold and the bandits ride away, the leader calls out, 'I am Joaquin. Joaquin, the avenger. Remember me.' He does not say Murieta then, either."

"Just the same, it's Joaquin Murieta who is the famous bandit. He's the one they write about on all the posters," insisted Pierre. After a moment he added, "What happened the next morning?"

"In the morning they went away," concluded Angel. "Joaquin and Rosita left for the gold fields. He said they had seen enough of San Francisco. They said I could go with them then, but I didn't."

Again he had come to another part of the story he did not wish to speak about: of finding his difficult way back to the boardinghouse; of his meeting with Mr. Schmidt, who, discovering Mamacita gone, had thrown Angel out into the street; of the miserable days wandering around hungry, lonely, frightened, until he had fallen in with a group of orphans like himself who had taken him into their little band.

"But if you had gone with them, you would never

have met me," pointed out Pierre triumphantly. "So you see it is better that you did not go."

Angel nodded. Yes, it was better. He would not have wanted to miss knowing Pierre and having him as a friend. For the past three years the two had been inseparable. They shared everything with each other— everything but the stories of how they came to be deserted. It was an unwritten law among the waifs of San Francisco that this subject was never discussed.

"But that is how I know Joaquin will welcome us," he concluded. "He is my friend, and he asked me to come. And you will be welcome too, Pierre."

"I'll have to think about it." Pierre's thin mouth set in a line of unusual stubbornness. He began stowing leftover food into his pocket as he looked out over the bay. "The fog is lifting," he announced. "But I think it's too early for the Catcher to be out. He likes afternoons best. Let's go down to the square."

To Angel and Pierre, Portsmouth Square, which some of the old-timers still called The Plaza, was the most exciting place in the world. It was a dusty, hard-trodden area, marked off from the streets by a low fence, and surrounded by saloons and gambling houses. Three years ago, these establishments were housed in tents or hastily thrown up wooden shacks, but there had been a great surge of construction, and the buildings surrounding the square were now more substantial. Some were even faced with stone, while others had verandas running like sashes across their second stories, and heavy shutters which could be closed to keep driving sand from pitting their plate-glass windows.

The boys had never been inside one of these magnificent palaces. Everyone knew that the waifs of San Francisco lived by theft and begging—how could they exist otherwise?—so guards were posted to keep them out. But through the windows and when the doors were flung wide, they had had glimpses of the interiors. On the walls were beautiful pictures in gold frames, and long mirrors which reflected the light of crystal chandeliers. The huge rooms were crowded with people milling around or sitting at the many small tables gambling, and there were always the sounds of music and laughter and of people having a good time.

Of course, you had to be very close to a doorway to hear these sounds of enjoyment, for outdoors they were absorbed by the louder noises of the bands that played in the square behind the fence. Since the bands played twenty-four hours every day but Sunday, it required several different organizations to maintain the schedule. One band in particular was Angel's favorite. It was directed by his friend Jake Plumber, who sometimes asked the boy to sing along with the musicians. He was always rewarded with a coin afterward, but although Angel accepted it gratefully, he would have sung for nothing. He liked to sing, and it was especially gratifying to have all the important horns and instruments take second place to his own voice.

As they arrived this morning, he was delighted to see that it was Jake Plumber's musicians who were performing. He grabbed Pierre's arm and spoke close to his ear above the noises of the square.

"I'm going over to the band. They might ask me to sing."

"Walk with me first," coaxed Pierre. "Just a couple of turns around the square."

A turn around the square was fun, too, so Angel decided the band would wait.

Day and night, the walks before the buildings were thronged with people. Although they were mostly men, there was an occasional woman, usually beautifully dressed and smelling of perfume. There were red-shirted miners from the diggings; Mexicans with wide-brimmed sombreros and bright serapes thrown over their shoulders; soldiers in dusty uniforms, jangling spurs on their boots and sabers at their sides; pig-tailed Chinese, who never lifted their eyes from their black-slippered, shuffling feet; blanketed Indians and Indians proudly wearing cast-off remnants of white men's clothing; sailors from a newly deserted ship in the bay, bent on quicker returns from the mines; gamblers in tall silk hats, sometimes decorated with a squirrel's tail or a cluster of jangling bells; Australians; South Americans; Frenchmen; Germans; Englishmen, and men from every part of the United States. Around and around the four sides of the square they paraded, enjoying the thin warmth of the sun, which had won its battle against the fog. At the moment they were reveling in the excitement of being here, but in the back of every man's mind was a single thought: the gold that he hoped to wrestle from the California earth.

Pierre grasped Angel's arm in excitement.

"Look! Just ahead of us. Two or three up. It's Sam Brannan. And there's a bulge in his back pocket."

"No," objected Angel. "Not Sam Brannan. He's too sharp. He'd catch you at it."

16

"In this crowd?" Pierre laughed away the idea. "The way they're jammed up and pushing?"

"Sam Brannan's on the council. He's the one who always stirs up the people into doing things, like forming the Vigilantes. There probably wouldn't even be an orphan asylum if it wasn't for him. Take somebody new in town. They wouldn't be looking for a hand in their pocket."

"Sam Brannan's rich," argued Pierre recklessly. "He owns a newspaper and a mill and I don't know what all. In this crowd I can lift the tail of his coat and have his wallet out in a second. He'll never know a thing. Coming?"

"No." Angel shook his head. "I'm going over to the band."

"Suit yourself." Pierre squeezed ahead of the men in front of them and in a few seconds had disappeared in the crowd.

Angel continued on for a few paces, then he stepped off the walk, crossing over to the dusty square where the brass band was playing furiously. He didn't know why he felt so uneasy. Pierre was the cleverest of them all.

Chapter 2

As soon as Angel reached the spot where the band was playing he forgot all about Pierre. He stood listening to the music they produced, silently admiring the flash of sunlight on the gold and silver horns and the masterful way of the drummer, who often gave his sticks a twirl before striking them against the taut head of his instrument. The fact that it was loud, at close range almost earsplitting, did not bother him. It was music, and all music stirred something within him.

The band finished its selection and Jake Plumber, turning to bow to the small group that had wandered over to listen close at hand, saw Angel standing there. He smiled and beckoned.

"Come up and sing a few choruses. We'll do 'Oh! Susanna.' Been a good half hour since we give them that."

As Angel stepped forward eagerly, Jake spoke to his men.

"Remember to keep it down, boys. Sweet, soft background, that's what's called for when you work with a singer. Don't blow your lungs out. The Injuns 'cross the bay at Oak Grove ain't listening anyhow."

He lifted his baton, and as it fell the musicians began the introduction to the favorite song of the gold miners. Angel's eyes were on Jake's face, and when the leader nodded he began to sing.

> "Oh, I come from Salem City
> With my washbowl on my knee
> And I'm going to California
> The gold rush for to see.
> It rained all night the day I left
> The weather it was dry
> The sun so hot I froze myself
> Oh, brothers, don't you cry."

His voice was high and sweet. Every note was clear and true, and the bandsmen, following instructions, provided a muted accompaniment. There were several verses to the song and Angel sang them all. When he finished there was applause from the handful of listeners, and some of them tossed coins on the ground before the singer. Angel scurried to pick them up, being careful to give them all to Jake Plumber. If he pocketed any himself, he might not be invited to sing again.

"One moment. One moment, there."

Jake had accepted the coins and was turning once more to his musicians when he was interrupted by a member of the audience. A man had stepped forward and was holding him firmly by the sleeve of his coat.

"Let the boy sing again," ordered the stranger. "We've had enough of your blasting and blaring and thumping. I wish to hear the boy."

Plumber's face turned red.

"I don't know who you are, mister," he said angrily. "But my band here's one of the finest in this city. We're hired to play music for so many hours every day. If you don't like it—"

Angel stared at the man who dared speak so rudely to Mr. Plumber. He was of middle height, with a neatly trimmed brown beard and flashing hazel eyes. He wore a tailed coat that was neat and clean but a little threadbare and a tall hat like the gamblers wore. But he wasn't a gambler. Angel was sure of that, although he couldn't have told how he knew.

Obviously the man was a stranger to San Francisco or he would have known about the bands playing in the square and the respect due the bandmaster. But he didn't have the look of those newly arrived by the overland route. Their skin was always burned red by the sun, and there were lines about their eyes from squinting against wind and dust. He couldn't have stepped off one of the ships that made the long voyage around the Horn either. His strong, white teeth were not loosened by scurvy, and he stood firmly, commandingly, in his black boots.

Then the stranger solved the mystery himself. He smiled at Jake Plumber, and the voice, which had been brusque, underwent a change. It was a rich voice and, although the words were spoken, it was almost as though he were singing, for his tones ran the gamut of a musical score. Sometimes they seemed to throb, like the deepest notes of the bass, then they grew light with the sweetness of a clarinet. Angel heard him with amazement, and even Jake Plumber must have been impressed, for he stood openmouthed.

"I beg your pardon, sir. Allow me to introduce myself. I am Thaddeus Joshua Quin, and I only arrived in your fair city yesterday, having come by packet ship down the coast from Oregon. I am a professor of music and elocution, and since we both follow the same art, music, I am sure you will understand my excitement on hearing the pitch, the tone, the range, of that extraordinary voice. I was so carried away by it that everything else was forgotten. As an artist yourself and the discoverer of this great talent, perhaps you will understand my emotions and overlook my unforgivable remarks about your own distinguished group of musicians."

The red began fading slowly from Jake's face, but, although he closed his mouth, he continued to stare at Professor Quin with some doubt. Angel nodded to himself. The stranger's appearance had a simple explanation after all. A sea trip down the coast from Oregon was too short to contract scurvy.

"As a great favor from one artist to another," continued Professor Quin, "would your group render another number in which the boy might participate?"

"I don't know if we can." Jake scratched his bristly chin. "Never tried out another with him. I don't 'spect Angel knows the words to too many songs. Maybe 'Yankee Doodle.' We could try that. Or we could run through 'Susanna' once more. The customers never get tired of it."

"No, no," objected Professor Quin hastily. "I do not wish to put you out. And if the boy does not know the words, it might reflect on your own musicianship. It might make your artists look bad, you understand. Do you mean to tell me, sir, that your group must play on and on without stopping to rest all day? The thought is brutal! An insult to the arts!"

"Oh, we take a few minutes off now and then," admitted Jake. "Got to get the wind back, you might say."

"And aptly put," agreed Professor Quin. His eyes traveled from one to another of the bandsmen, now beginning to perspire slightly in the morning sun, and he shook his head. "Let them rest for a moment now," he pleaded sympathetically. "For the sake of art and to conserve their talent. And while they are resting, perhaps the boy will render us a song of his own choosing."

"Well—" Jake hesitated, but at the professor's nods of encouragement he gave in. "Set or stretch for a couple of minutes boys," he called to his musicians.

"Now, lad." Professor Quin turned briskly to Angel. "Sing something for me. Something of your own choosing, but with as wide a range as possible."

Angel looked at him helplessly. He did not know what to sing.

"Music soothes in sorrow, tranquilizes the passion, and wears away the irritabilities of life," prompted Professor Quin. "The soul drinks in more deeply the saddening sweetness when it breaks into the soft, low notes of song. Sweetly, boy, sweetly. None of that washboard-on-my-knee claptrap."

It was obvious that Professor Quin did not care for the songs of the miners, and the only others Angel knew were those from home. He began one that the wives of fishermen sang in Valparaiso when their men were at sea. It was a little too sad for the tastes of the people here in San Francisco, and he was not even sure that he remembered all the words, but since they were in Spanish he could substitute without detection.

He was not allowed to finish, however, for right in the middle, Mr. Sam Brannan came striding across the square toward them. Even from a distance they could see that his face was red with anger.

"Enough! Enough!" Jake Plumber stopped Angel hastily as he waved to his bandsmen. "Back to work, boys. 'Little Brown Jug,' and give it everything you got."

"This is outrageous," protested Professor Quin. "You stopped him on high C."

"There he is! That's another of the young scamps. Grab him!" called Mr. Brannan, pointing with a gold-headed stick in the direction of Angel. "If I have to round up every one of these blasted orphans by myself, and it looks like I will, I'll do it."

A second man, previously obscured by the splendor of the councilman, darted out from behind Mr. Brannan and lunged forward. Angel saw him coming and stepped aside. A second later he would have been free to lose himself in the crowd, but Professor Quin put out one black boot and Angel tripped, tumbling to the ground.

"Thank you, sir," panted the man, reaching out, but Professor Quin pushed him away indignantly. He himself helped Angel to his feet then, with his left arm

encircling the boy to hold him fast, he stood confronting the newcomers.

"Who are you?" he demanded. "And by what right do you interrupt a young artist in the performance of his art?"

"My name's Sam Brannan, and I'm a member of the council." The big man frowned slightly. "And I interrupt, as you call it, in pursuit of duty. We've got a new ordinance in this town. All orphans are to be housed in the city orphan asylum, where they'll be taught the meaning of law and decency. And high time, too. Not five minutes ago, I caught one of the young rapscallions red-handed while he was trying to pick my pocket."

Angel felt a heavy feeling rise inside his chest. Pierre! Pierre had been caught! Even now he must be on his

way to the orphan asylum on the hill. There was no
means of escape, he was sure of that. So many of the
children had gone unwillingly that guards were on duty,
at least for a time.

"This boy is an orphan?" asked Professor Quin.
"What is your name, lad?"

"Angel."

"Angel what?"

"Angel Palma." He had to think for a moment before
he answered. It had been three years since anyone had
asked his last name.

"He has a great talent," announced Professor Quin,
and his amazing voice was like the fanfare of trumpets.
"A beautiful voice. A God-given talent. I know. I am
an authority. What provision is made in your orphan
asylum for instruction in music, sir?"

"Why, none that I know of." Sam Brannan seemed surprised. "Oh, I suppose they sing sometimes. Nothing to stop them. What we want to stop is this thievery. They pick that up from each other, those that are old enough. Some of the little ones just beg, but they'll come to stealing soon enough if we don't take a hand. The babies starve. We've got lots of them. Deserted babies nearly every week."

"Unfortunate," agreed Professor Quin, but he seemed to be thinking of something else.

Angel moved tentatively under the arm that held him. If Professor Quin would just loosen his grip, he might be able to get away. It would be lonely without Pierre, but he'd rather be by himself than shut up in an orphan asylum.

"We treat them well," explained Mr. Brannan gruffly. "They get proper food and clothes to keep them warm. We're hiring a teacher so they can even learn reading and ciphering, and they'll learn honest work."

"But no music," objected Professor Quin sadly. "Food for the flesh, but none for the soul. Mr. Brannan, I will take this boy off your hands. It is my duty. He has a great talent, and doubtless fate led my steps here today for just that purpose. I will cultivate the ground about the seed. I will nurture it, as do the sun and rain, from my own wealth of experience."

"Hold your horses there," objected Sam Brannan. "That boy may be an orphan, but he's a human being. He's entitled to what the city's prepared to give him. I don't know you or anything about you. Maybe turning the boy over to you is not the thing to do at all."

"Quite right. Entirely proper." Professor Quin's tone

changed. It became warm and glowing. "Allow me to introduce myself, sir. I am Thaddeus Joshua Quin, recently of Oregon, but formerly of the state of Illinois. I am a professor of music and elocution in that settlement beside the beautiful falls of the Willamette, Oregon City. Until recently, I owned a nearby donation land claim of six hundred and forty acres. I will be in your city only until four o'clock this afternoon when, with my wife and daughter, I will take the boat to Sacramento, and thence to the gold fields. I propose to take this boy with me as my pupil and protégé."

"Your wife and daughter, eh?" repeated Sam Brannan. "Well, that sounds a little better. Although I'd feel better if I could see them with my own eyes."

"So you may, if you care to be at the dock to see us off this afternoon," invited Professor Quin cordially. "Mrs. Quin and my daughter are remaining in our room until the time for departure. There is a certain element in your city—forgive me for mentioning it—which might prove distasteful to ladies of breeding."

"The diggings won't be much better," said Brannan dryly. He looked sharply at Angel. "Well, how about it, boy? You want to go with this man?"

Angel's mind had been racing ever since he heard the words "gold fields." Of course this wasn't the way he had planned to go, or the company he had selected. But Pierre was gone. Angel could do nothing to help him now. If he accompanied the Quins, his expenses would be taken care of. Anyone who volunteered to assume responsibility for an orphan must be very rich. Besides, Angel wouldn't have to be alone. And as soon

27

as they arrived, he would run away and find his friend Joaquin Murieta.

He looked at Sam Brannan eagerly.

"Oh yes, sir. I do want to go with him."

"All right. I guess you're old enough to speak for yourself," agreed Brannan. Then he added pointedly. "I'll look for you all at the boat landing this afternoon."

Chapter 3

Professor Quin knocked three times on the closed door, then leaned down to speak through the keyhole.

"It is your husband, madam, Thaddeus Joshua Quin. It is quite safe to open the door."

Angel looked around curiously. It was the first time he had ever been inside a hotel. This was one of San Francisco's newer buildings, termed by the professor as "a decent, respectable establishment." Compared with the Portsmouth House and some of the more elaborate structures close to the square, it was disappointingly plain, with uncarpeted floors and walls painted in a practical shade of saffron. It smelled of raw wood and lye soap.

As Professor Quin straightened up, Angel could hear the sounds of a heavy object being dragged across the floor. Then there was the rasp of an iron key in the lock, and finally the door was opened cautiously and an eye appeared in the small crack.

"It's all right," announced a high voice. "It is Papa."

"Quite so, Rowena," approved Professor Quin, signaling that Angel was to follow as he stepped inside.

The moment they were across the threshold the girl who had admitted them shut the door hastily and turned the key.

"Shall we push the bureau back?" she asked anxiously.

"That will not be necessary, Rowena." He smiled at her with affection. "Only when you and your mother are alone must we take the extra precaution of the bureau against the door. I am here now to protect you."

Angel stared at the girl curiously. She was taller than he by half a head, and plump. Her brown hair was parted exactly in the center and braided into two thick plaits which hung nearly to her waist. She had a small nose which tilted at the end, eyes of exactly the same shade and shape as Professor Quin's, and a wide mouth which first dropped open in astonishment at the sight of the strange boy but immediately turned up in a delighted smile of welcome.

"I have brought a surprise," announced the professor. "This is Angel Palma, the possessor of one of the truest, most extraordinary voices that it has ever been my privilege to hear. Angel, this is my wife, Mrs. Quin, and my daughter, Rowena."

Angel bobbed his head shyly, and Rowena tittered.

"Angel's a funny name," she observed frankly.

"Mind your manners," ordered her mother, frowning. "There are those who say your own name is not so usual."

"Oh, I know that," Rowena admitted quickly. "That's why it's nice to meet somebody with a funnier one. My name comes from a book," she added confidentially to Angel. "Papa read about it in Sir Walter Scott's novel *Ivanhoe*. The Lady Rowena was the—"

"That will do," interrupted Professor Quin. "There will be ample time later on to discuss the origin of your name. Angel comes from Chile, and no doubt his name is most usual in that country. We will say no more about it. We will pretend that this interlude in our conversation did not occur."

"Yes, Papa," agreed Rowena.

"How do you do, Angel," said Mrs. Quin politely, and Angel turned from Rowena, whom he already disliked, to examine her more closely.

Mrs. Quin was not a great deal taller than her daughter, but she was very slight. Her bones seemed to be close to her fair skin, giving her a drawn, taut look. She had the same brown hair, but it was done up in a knot on her head, and her eyes were brown, not hazel. She wore a long, black dress with a small collar of homemade tatting. Angel found his eyes wandering to the thin hands below the small, neat cuffs. They were red, with large knuckles and roughened skin, and seemed out of place on such a lady as Mrs. Quin.

"I heard him singing with a miserable band in the center of town," explained Professor Quin. "It was like a shaft of radiant moonlight in the midst of a thunderstorm. Such clarity! Such trueness of pitch, even in all that caterwauling, and despite the abomination of the lyrics."

"Really, Thaddeus?" Mrs. Quin smiled at her husband indulgently. "So you brought him here so he could sing for Rowena and me. That was thoughtful."

"You misunderstand me, Almira." Professor Quin seemed surprised. "I rescued him from a soulless institution where his great talents would be stifled. Under my tutorage, they will thrive and flourish. I will bring out the hidden promise of that rich voice, which will someday thrill the world. Angel is my protégé, and, naturally, he must accompany us."

"You mean he's to come with us?" repeated Mrs. Quin in dismay. "But Thaddeus, have you thought what it will mean? Another mouth to feed? Just now?"

"All that will be taken care of." He brushed her protests away airily. "Once we get there, we can gather up enough nuggets the first day to feed a dozen orphans. Two dozen. A man whom I encountered on the square this morning told me that a friend of his was traveling through the Mother Lode, determining where to stake his claim, and he sat down on a rock to rest. Would you believe it, Almira, that rock was solid gold?"

"In some places the streets are filled with it, Mama." Rowena added her own arguments to those of her father. "It sticks to your shoes when you walk around. I don't suppose every place is like that, though," she added thoughtfully. "Probably just one or two towns. Or they wouldn't need all those gold pans and shovels."

"Exactly." The professor turned to smile his approval. "What we must do is travel to the right place. The Mother Lode. We won't waste our time on any of the smaller veins which straggle out to the sides."

Angel had never been to the gold fields, but he had heard enough about them to know that gold did not yield itself so easily. When he looked at Mrs. Quin he could tell that she didn't think so either, but she did not argue with her husband. Instead, she brought the subject back to him.

"Have you asked the boy anything about himself? Even though he is an orphan, there may be other relatives."

Angel shook his head quickly. Since Mrs. Quin seemed reluctant to have him along, she might convince her husband that it was their duty to put him on a boat bound for Chile. Angel had nothing against his aunts and uncles and cousins in Valparaiso. He had been fond of them once, but that was a long time ago. Now, Joaquin Murieta, the bandit whose fame had traveled the length and breadth of California, had assumed far more importance in his mind.

"How long have you been an orphan?" demanded Mrs. Quin.

"Many years," said Angel, making his voice sad and helpless. "I was only a little boy when it happened. We had just come to San Francisco. Gold had not been discovered long."

"Only a baby." The professor's voice throbbed with pity. "Why, he can't be more than ten now. Look at him measured against Rowena there, and she's twelve. That gives me two full years to cultivate and train that glorious voice. Naturally, I shall not allow him to sing a note once he is twelve. Permitting a lad to sing between the ages of twelve and sixteen is ruinous to the mature voice which will emerge later."

Angel barely caught himself in time. He had been about to correct the professor's estimate of his age.

"You are right, sir. I am ten," he said meekly. How lucky that Professor Quin had voiced his theory early, and what a crazy idea it was anyway. Whoever heard of not allowing boys to sing whenever they wanted to, regardless of their ages?

"How did your folks die?" Mrs. Quin's brown eyes fixed themselves upon his face. There was no sympathy here, although both her husband and daughter were shaking their heads sadly.

"It was the water." Angel took quick inspiration from the pitcher and bowl atop the commode across the room. "The spring water in San Francisco is very bad. They say that ten men die every day from drinking it."

"Goodness," gasped Rowena. "I just had a drink. Part of a drink. It tasted funny, so I spit most of it out."

Even Mrs. Quin looked at the water pitcher uneasily.

"Ten out of a population of forty thousand is not high," soothed the professor. "And we cannot be sure it was the water. It could have been something else, Almira."

"It will do to wash in, anyway," she decided. "There's soap in the dish. Get some of that grime off your hands and face, young man. I want to see what's under it."

Angel stared at her blankly. Then Rowena pulled on his sleeve and led him over to the commode. She poured water from the pitcher into the bowl and indicated a towel hanging next to it.

"Mama wants you to wash," she explained. "You'll get used to it if you come with us."

Angel picked up the soap and dipped it gingerly into the bowl. He was enduring a great deal just to get to Joaquin, he decided.

"How did you live all these years?" Mrs. Quin was not yet through with her questions.

As he rolled the soap in his dampened hands, Angel considered telling her the truth. It would be fun to see the scandalized horror on that prim, tight face. Just in time he remembered that not many people would be willing to take a thief into their family group.

"Sometimes they paid me a few cents for singing with the bands," he explained. "Or I might get a penny for running an errand for a rich man. Sometimes the hotels threw out leftovers. Anybody can sleep in the ships in the harbor. Nobody cares about that."

"Brave little lad!" Professor Quin blew his nose on a large, white handkerchief. "My heart aches for the suffering he has endured. But never fear, lad. It is behind you now, though not forgotten. Adversity strengthens every character. It adds fuel to the flame of genius."

"He's like some of the people in the stories, isn't he, Papa?" asked Rowena sympathetically. "They had to suffer and suffer before the fairy godmother or the king or somebody came to their rescue. Then they lived happily ever after."

"You're not through washing yet," warned Mrs. Quin crisply as Angel reached for the towel. "It's going to take a lot more scrubbing to get through all that dirt. But it might be a good idea to change the water in the bowl."

Above the commode was a small mirror. It was the first time Angel had seen his own face for several years, and as the dirt reluctantly gave way beneath the soap and water, it was like observing a stranger.

His hair was dark. He had known that, for occasionally he or Pierre had borrowed a knife to cut each other's hair. When he left Valparaiso, his cheeks had been plump. Now they were thin, and his inquisitive eyes seemed larger than he remembered. He was paler too, for the fogs and thin sunlight of San Francisco did not burn his skin the way the hot sun of Valparaiso had. Mamacita had often said they had Spanish blood, blended with only a little of the Araucanian, the Indian, and as Angel stared at the reflection in the mirror, he could see that it was true. The straight nose, the thin lips, the pale skin of this stranger staring back at him could be those of a Spaniard or an Italian, even of a Frenchman like Pierre.

"If you can leave off admiring yourself, that will do for now," Mrs. Quin spoke sharply. "Wipe dry, then come and let me look at you."

Angel dropped the soap back into its dish and hurried to obey. The towel was harsh and scratchy, and when he finished drying himself, it was stained.

"Cold water just won't do the job," decided Mrs. Quin as she inspected his efforts. "But there's no way to heat it here in this room. I don't dare look at your ears, knowing what I'm sure to find." She turned to her husband. "Thaddeus, if you're bound to take this boy along, we'll have to get him something decent to wear. These clothes aren't even fit for scrub rags. I doubt if I could get the smell out even by boiling."

"Is that what it is?" Professor Quin's nose wrinkled with distaste. "It wasn't so apparent in the open air, but ever since we closed the door—"

Angel grew warm with anger. Who did these people think they were, anyway? Going around making remarks about how others smelled. Everybody had an odor; they

were just different, that's all. Pierre and the other orphans smelled just as he did. After a while you didn't even notice it.

"I will take him out at once and purchase proper garments," offered Professor Quin. "New clothing for a small boy cannot come too dear, even in this city of extravagant prices."

"Oh, no, Thaddeus," objected his wife, getting to her feet. "Remember our bargain. I make all the purchases and handle all the money."

"Really, Almira!" He frowned in annoyance. "This is carrying things too far. It is ridiculous. Degrading. Besides, the streets of San Francisco are not fit for gentle ladies of your breeding."

"I'll have to chance it. And you'll be there to protect us," she reminded him firmly. "Get your bonnet, Rowena. We can't leave you here alone. We'll all have to go."

Angel swallowed his anger. As long as they wanted to buy him new clothes, the reason they gave for the purchase didn't matter. The piecemeal garments that he wore were either too large or too small, and his boots were falling off his feet. He wished Pierre could know that he was finally getting new boots.

Although Professor Quin had many suggestions and comments, it did not take Angel long to realize that it was his wife who made the final decisions. Since they were strangers in San Francisco, she asked the boy to recommend a shop where they could make their purchases.

"And one that doesn't price things sky-high," she added quickly. "We're not made of money."

Ah, but you have plenty of it, thought Angel bitterly. Money for the boat passage from Oregon, money to stay in a hotel, money to buy new clothes for a stranger. He led them to the shop where Pierre had recently acquired his new boots. Any merchant who stocked one pair of small-sized boots possibly might stock two.

Professor Quin requested a suit in Angel's size, something decent and serviceable along the lines of the one he himself was wearing. Immediately Mrs. Quin objected, saying that two-piece suits came far too dear. A sturdy pair of breeches and a jacket were quite good enough for a boy to wear to the mines.

"Maybe I should have blue jeans and a red shirt," suggested Angel, trying to keep his voice innocent of the scorn he felt. Why were rich people always so stingy? "They're even cheaper, and it's what miners wear."

For the first time Mrs. Quin regarded him with something close to approval.

"Show us some of those," she agreed promptly. "And a suit of underdrawers. One will be plenty, for I can wash them out when I do ours. And a pair of socks and some boots."

When the storekeeper had filled their order, the bill came to $46.25. Mrs. Quin gasped. Her eyes sought her husband, but he was no longer interested. He had led Rowena to the front of the shop and was pointing out some of the sights of the city through the opening.

Angel grinned. Even though they had bought the cheapest things possible, it was a lot of money. It would serve her right if he just stood there and let her pay. But then, there was the shopkeeper to consider. Angel had no love for rich merchants either. Why let him get away with something? He came and stood behind Mrs. Quin, lifting his head to whisper in her ear.

"Bargain with him."

She jumped and looked over her shoulder.

"Offer him twenty-five," whispered Angel, frowning with impatience. Surely anyone ought to know enough not to take the first price that was asked. A couple of years ago all goods had been sold by auction to the highest bidders, but recently auctions had fallen off in popularity. Only bargaining remained.

Mrs. Quin's brain was sharp. She caught on to the idea immediately.

"I'll give you twenty-five," she announced crisply.

The shopkeeper lowered his price a little, and Mrs. Quin raised her bid slightly. In the end, she paid $37.50 for the small pile of boy's clothing, and as she handed it to Angel to carry, it was accompanied by a reserved smile.

Once outside the shop, Professor Quin consulted a large watch attached to a long, gold chain from his waistcoat pocket.

"The hours speed by on winged feet," he told them. "It approaches three o'clock."

"Then we'd best get back to the hotel," decided Mrs. Quin. "We're all packed up, and the lunch basket's filled, though I must say, Thaddeus, it cost a heap of money. I hope things'll be more reasonable once we get to the mines. I feel like I'm eating gold every time I bite into an apple. We'll let the boy change his clothes, then we had best get down to the wharf."

"Exactly what I had in mind." His hazel eyes sparkled with excitement. "Like knights of old, we must be on with our quest, eh, Rowena?"

"Oh, yes, Papa." Rowena smiled happily. "It's sort of like we're Sir Galahad seeking the Golden Grail, isn't it?"

40

"Holy Grail, child," reproved her father. "Not Golden. You must learn to be correct in your comparisons."

Angel looked at them curiously. He had come to the conclusion that Professor Quin was a little touched in the head, and it was evident that the weakness ran in the family.

But they were right about one thing. He had never known an hour to go by so fast. When they reached the hotel, the two small trunks were pushed out into the hall. Mrs. Quin and Rowena each sat on one, with the lunch basket between them, while the professor and Angel remained in the room. Washing his hands and face had not been enough. He was required to take a cold sponge bath before he was permitted to put on the new clothes. They felt strange and stiff, and he looked a little wistfully at the old ones in the corner. Maybe they were ragged and smelled a little, but they were his. He hated to leave them behind.

A cart had been hired to take them to the dock, and it was waiting when they came outside. Mrs. Quin and Rowena squeezed into the seat with the driver, while Angel and the professor rode behind with the baggage. As they bounced along through the loose sand and ruts, the boy looked from side to side. Everything seemed different when viewed from the elevation of a cart, or perhaps it was the scratchy, new clothes that gave him such an odd sensation. He felt like a stranger in a strange town, embarking on a frightening adventure.

Once they reached the dock and he could jump down to feel the rough planks beneath his creaking new boots, he was himself again. He had seen these river schooners before. Often he and Pierre had stood and watched as

41

they cast off, their decks crowded with hopeful prospectors headed for Sutter's Fort, which had become the thriving town of Sacramento. It was a pleasant sight, for everyone was gay and excited, but Angel had never expected to be one of the passengers. He looked up at Professor Quin, momentarily grateful to the man who was paying his fare.

Holding Mrs. Quin and Rowena by their elbows and signaling with his head that Angel was to follow, the professor ascended the wobbly gangplank. With many "Excuse me, sirs" and "I beg your pardons," he secured them places at the rail.

"Ah, there he is!" he exclaimed in sudden surprise. "I had quite forgotten the fellow. Wave, my dear. Wave, Rowena. That is the gentleman to whom I promised the honor of an introduction. For a time he questioned my authority in assuming responsibility for my new protégé."

Angel stared across the narrow strip of muddy water separating the schooner from the dock. Sam Brannan was there, as he had said he would be, rising half a head above most of the crowd. His eyes had already found them on deck, and as the ladies waved obediently, he removed his glossy hat and smiled.

Angel glared back at him. Someday, he told himself, when he had found Joaquin Murieta, the two of them would return and make Sam Brannan pay for what he had done to Pierre.

Chapter 4

Angel woke up all at once, and immediately wished that he hadn't. His body felt sore and cramped, because he had slept on the hard deck wound up into as tight a ball as he could manage. He had been trying to protect himself from the clouds of mosquitoes that appeared just before dusk. Now as he straightened his aching legs, he realized that the hum of mosquitoes had vanished, but that his tender skin beneath the new clothes was itching in a hundred places. Fleas! He sat up, scratching vigorously.

The eastern sky was flooded with pink, but it was still too early to make out much of the countryside on either bank of the river. He could hear the splash of the water against the revolving wooden paddles and the pounding of the overworked engine below. That engine, brought from France, was a wonderful thing, for it meant that the vessel need not rely on wind or currents. But it had its drawbacks. For one thing, it made the whole schooner throb and shake so much that Angel wondered how it held together.

The deck was littered with long, dark mounds which were sleeping men bound for the gold fields. Now that he knew about the mosquitoes, Angel understood why so many passengers had brought lengths of canvas and old blankets aboard. These were the returning miners who had made this river trip before. As soon as it was dusk, they had wrapped themselves into cocoons, leaving only air holes for their noses. Only the inexperienced, like Angel and the Quins, would arrive swollen with itching bites.

He grinned as he thought of Mrs. Quin. By now she would be wishing that she had parted with the extra money for one of the small cabins below. There were two other ladies aboard, and they had not quibbled over the expense. They had been glad to pay and not sleep in the open. But Mrs. Quin, clutching her large black handbag, had insisted that the charge was already too high. She would not squander one penny more.

It was growing lighter by the moment, and all around him the passengers were awakening. Scratching and grumbling, they staggered to their feet, most of them making their way to the railing around the deck. Angel stood up, reeling a little from the reverberation of the engine, and went there too.

The river was cutting through a great valley. There were bushes and trees on either side, but no signs of habitation. Against the fading pink sky, he could see the dark outlines of hills or mountains, remote and seemingly far away.

All the men were excited. Angel could tell by their conversations that they were glad it was morning, which meant that they were nearly at the end of this stage of their journey. There was talk about "diggings" and "strikes" and "pan-outs" and "color," words which had only little meaning for him now, but which he stowed away carefully in his mind because someday they might.

It was easy to tell the new prospectors from the old. The experienced miners, returning from a spree in the big city, were the authorities. Their advice was eagerly sought, and they were only too glad to give information.

Weber, of Weber's Creek, had taken $50,000 in only a few weeks. At Dry Diggings, near Coloma, a fellow named Wilson scraped up $2000 in nuggets under the door of his shack. Five men on Feather River made $75,000 in three months. But when the old prospectors were pressed, they admitted that they themselves did not have claims on Weber's Creek or Dry Diggings or Feather River. They were prospecting around Hangtown or Chinese Camp or Mariposa. They had only given out these startling facts as an indication of what the whole country might produce. They themselves got by and couldn't complain, but the big strikes were elsewhere. They advised the newcomers to look farther on.

The conversations were so interesting that Angel was almost resentful when the professor arrived and touched him on the arm. The Quins were about to eat their breakfast out of the lunch basket. If Angel was hungry he had better come now, for Mrs. Quin wanted to get everything repacked before they docked at Sacramento.

Long experience had taught Angel to eat whenever food was available, so he followed the professor with only a backward glance toward the miners. When they arrived, Mrs. Quin was sitting on a coil of rope, and Rowena was teetering on the throbbing deck beside her.

"The floor feels bouncy," announced Rowena. "I feel like I'm going to fall down."

"Then sit before you do," advised her mother shortly. "Did you find out when we'll arrive, Thaddeus? I can't stand much more of this."

"Soon. Soon," the professor told her soothingly. "You will feel better when you have something in your stomach, Almira."

Angel looked at Mrs. Quin closely. As he had expected, her face was red and swollen with bites. There were dark circles under her eyes too, evidence that she had spent a sleepless night. For some reason he didn't enjoy the spectacle as much as he had expected.

"You'll all have to go easy on the food." Obviously she had already made up her mind on this point, for she immediately handed each of them a small slab of bread and half an apple.

Angel accepted his share without comment. He had eaten smaller breakfasts than this many times. But the professor was outraged.

"Really, madam," he protested. "With a full lunch basket, there is no need to be so saving. What kind of a meal is this for a grown man?"

"It's an expensive meal, Thaddeus," she explained wearily. "Bread's a dollar a loaf, and apples a dollar apiece. The lunch basket's not full any more. We had supper out of it last night, and I don't know when we'll get to fill it again."

"When? Why, at Sacramento, of course." He frowned

impatiently. "There is no telling how long we shall be there before we find transportation to the Mother Lode."

"More expensive hotels! And meals! And goodness knows what our transportation will come to!" Mrs. Quin shook her head helplessly.

Angel turned away in disgust, carrying his breakfast. He supposed this was how rich people stayed rich. They parted with each penny with the greatest reluctance.

"Where are you going, Angel?" Professor Quin called after him.

"Back to the rail. I can eat there just as well as here." He felt sorry for the professor who was burdened with such a wife, so he managed to keep his tone civil.

"May I go with him, Papa? May I, Mama?" pleaded Rowena instantly. "I want to see over the side, too."

"Oh, I'm afraid not," began her father. "It would not be—"

"Let her go, Thaddeus." Surprisingly enough, Mrs. Quin came to Rowena's defense. "She'll be in plain view, so nothing can happen. And there'll be two of them. It isn't like she was alone. Besides, there's a few things I have to say to you in private."

"Oh, thank you, Mama." Rowena did not wait for her father's permission. She hurried after Angel as fast as the shaking deck would permit.

"Don't let her lean over, Angel," called Professor Quin anxiously. "And if anyone stops to speak to you, take her arm and escort her straight back to us."

Angel nodded. He didn't want Rowena's company, but there was nothing he could do about it. Perhaps she would soon tire of watching the shore line and the monotonous river and want to return to her parents. For

47

that reason he chose a spot at the rail where they were quite alone. If they stood close to the miners, Rowena might become interested in their talk and never leave.

"Isn't this exciting?" she demanded, hanging onto the railing and smiling over at him.

"You mean the mosquitoes? Or the fleas?" He stared significantly at her bumpy face. She must have slept on her side, for one cheek was swollen worse than the other. It gave her a curious, lopsided appearance.

"Fleas?" Immediately she began squirming inside her buttoned coat. "I didn't know there were fleas, too. I thought it was just the mosquito bites itching."

"Mosquitoes last night. Fleas this morning. The boat's crawling with them. Everybody on board is covered with fleas. Even your mother," he added deliberately.

She looked troubled.

"Poor Mama. You mustn't mind that she made you wash yourself yesterday. That's just the way she is. And you were a little dirty."

Angel stared down at the gray current without comment.

"This is very hard on Mama," insisted Rowena stubbornly. "She didn't want to come to California, you know. Papa's been talking about it for two years. He couldn't think about anything else. And so many other people we knew in Oregon were going to the gold mines. Every time one of them left, Papa would just talk about it and talk about it. So finally, when Mama saw how much it meant to him, she just had to give in. But she didn't want to come."

"Why did she then?" Angel looked at her angrily.

"Why didn't she just let him come by himself? Why didn't you two stay home?"

"We didn't have any place to stay," explained Rowena. She slid one hand between the buttons of her coat to scratch herself. "We had to sell the land, or there wouldn't have been any money to get here. I know it costs more for three passages than for one, but we have to live some place, Mama and me. She couldn't take out another claim. They don't let you have more than one. Besides, she'd never built a cabin. Papa did that, and he'll build us one here. Unless, of course, we find enough gold the first day to pay somebody to build one for us."

"You won't do that," Angel told her scornfully.

"We might," she insisted. "In the stories they do." Once again she smiled at him brightly. "Do you like stories?"

"Stories?"

"Yes. Papa and I do. He knows lots of them. He told me stories all the way across the plains. That was four years ago, when we left Illinois to come to Oregon. It was a long trip. It took from spring until late in the fall to get there. I don't think Mama wanted to go to Oregon much either. It was nice in Illinois. We had a real house, not a cabin made of logs. And Papa led the church choir, and gave singing and elocution lessons to young ladies."

"Elocution?" repeated Angel vaguely.

"That's learning to speak pieces. You know, poems," explained Rowena. "And the proper motions of your hands while you're speaking them. That's very important.

Papa knows all kinds of poems. He'll say some of them for you sometime, and then you'll see what I mean."

"Did people throw him money when he said the poems?" asked Angel, remembering the spectators in Portsmouth Square.

"No, no," objected Rowena quickly. "Papa taught other people how to say them. He's a professor, and he gave lessons. At least he did in Illinois. When we got to Oregon, it seemed nobody wanted lessons. That's why Mama decided we'd have to take out a donation land claim. Our money was all gone, and we had to live somehow."

Angel didn't know what a donation land claim was either, but he decided not to ask. Rowena's tone had been a little impatient when she explained about elocution.

"I think we're almost there," he told her, changing the subject.

Certainly the crowd of miners farther up the railing was behaving as though the end of the journey was in sight. The talk and laughter had grown louder, and some of them were pointing ahead. Others had left the group and were beginning to collect their piles of belongings on deck.

"Then we better go back to Mama and Papa," decided Rowena. "We don't want to get lost in a strange town."

Angel shrugged, but he followed her across the deck. He was sure it would be some time before the schooner docked, and equally sure that there was no danger of getting lost. But until he was safely arrived at the gold

fields and had found Joaquin, it would be just as well to keep on good terms with the Quins.

The wharf at Sacramento was a busy place these days. It had been enlarged from the small *embarcadero* built by Captain Sutter for the use of boats bringing supplies to his fort. The fort still stood on the rising ground above the river but it was deserted now; its employees all off at the mines. The morning sun picked flashes of light from the old brass cannon installed at the entrance as a silent threat against Indian raiders, but the Indians too were gone. It had not taken long for them to learn that the white man would pay equal weight in beans or beads for the yellow metal. Now they and their squaws and papooses were away searching busily.

Although Professor Quin could scarcely restrain himself, for the sake of the ladies, he permitted the miners to precede them down the gangplank.

"El Dorado," he kept saying to himself. "We are come to El Dorado."

Angel stared at him curiously. El Dorado meant "the gilded," but there was nothing gilded about the noisy, dusty wharf ahead of them. The passengers were shouting and jostling and pushing, just as they always did when they disembarked from a boat, and the people who greeted them were shouting and jostling and pushing too. The air was filled with dust, and everything looked a bit dingy.

As they reached the shore, a man squeezed through the crowd to grasp the professor's arm. He was coatless, and his yellow calico sleeves were held up by strips of ruffled cloth. A bowler hat was pushed well back on his head and seemed in perpetual danger of sliding off.

"Take the stage, sir. The Birch line goes everywhere. Shasta, Nevada City, Sonora. We'll get you there with speed and in greatest comfort. Stages leaving in just a few minutes. Where's your party bound for, sir? We've got a stage to every diggings you can name."

"A stage line? In this wilderness?" The professor seemed unable to believe his ears. "Did you hear, Almira? A stage line!"

"It would save tonight's hotel bill," calculated Mrs. Quin quickly. Clutching her black handbag tightly, she spoke to the man. "How much?"

" 'Pends on where you're bound for, lady." His darting eyes inspected her shrewdly, then seemed to settle on her handbag.

"The Mother Lode," announced Professor Quin in echoing tones.

"We can give you connections that'll take you clear to Mokelumne Hill. Can't get no deeper in the Mother Lode than that," promised the man.

"But how much?" persisted Mrs. Quin.

"You'll have to ask the driver." The yellow calico shoulders shrugged. "This way, if you please, folks. They're loading now."

For a moment Mrs. Quin held back.

"Oh, Thaddeus. It's sure to cost a lot."

"Even so, we cannot walk, Almira." Although his tone was sympathetic, the professor's hazel eyes were shining with excitement. "And by taking the stage now, we will save the night's lodging here in town."

"I suppose so." She sighed and permitted him to grasp her elbow once more. "Hold on to Papa's coat, Rowena. And tell the boy to walk close on your heels."

When they finally squeezed through the crowd and arrived at the area beyond, Angel caught his breath. He could scarcely believe his good fortune. Lined up awaiting passengers were five Concord stagecoaches!

Over a year ago he had seen the first of these magnificent coaches when it arrived in San Francisco and was proudly driven around Portsmouth Square. Since then, many of the larger ships from the East had carried one of the scarlet beauties in their holds. Some were for service in the two rival stage lines which left the square simultaneously at eight each morning, racing each other over sixty tortuous miles to the state capital at San Jose. Others had stood on the wharf for a few hours before they were rolled onto the decks of other vessels in the harbor.

More than once Angel and Pierre had speculated about the final destination of these coaches, and now he knew. They were for the use of the gold miners. Most important of all, he, who had never even dared to touch one with a finger in passing, was going to ride inside.

In the morning sunlight, the scarlet paint glittered and shone from a recent scrubbing, and the end coach was slightly turned so that he could see the miniature landscape painted on the door. The bodies were high off the road, and the running gear beneath was finished in a shade of sun-baked straw, a good color to hide road dust. The sides bulged slightly to give more room for inside passengers, and there was space for additional riders on the top. In the front was the driver's seat, a little higher than anyone else's, so he could look down on the muscular backs of his six-horse team.

"This is the Hangtown stage. You start with that,"

announced the man in the bowler hat proudly, pointing to one of the identical coaches. "No telling how you'll be routed yet, but the driver'll let you know. Where's your baggage?"

The professor's hand went to his forehead in a dramatic gesture.

"Still on the schooner. In the heat of excitement, it had momentarily slipped my mind."

"No harm done." The man grinned, showing a missing tooth. "Leave the missus here, and me and you'll go back after it. You and the young 'uns better take seats inside, ma'am," he advised Mrs. Quin. "You don't want it to fill up and take off without you."

"But where is the driver?" she protested. "It can't be that boy holding the horses. He's too young."

"No, ma'am. He's just a stablehand. You get in and set. Soon as the coach fills, the driver he'll show up. You can bet on that."

The seats were well padded, a luxury Angel had not expected, and there was ample room for nine passengers. Three of them, obviously miners, were already seated, waiting for the driver.

It was some time before they took off. Another miner came to occupy one of the two remaining seats, and from the thumping and bumping overhead, Angel was sure that some of the outside seats were being claimed. With much creaking and clattering and shouts from their drivers, two of the other stages pulled out, but theirs continued to wait quietly in the increasing heat.

Professor Quin returned in ample time to claim the last inside seat, but when Angel, who had decided that the closed coach would be stuffy, suggested that he would enjoy riding on top, the professor shook his head.

"I have plans which require your presence here," he said, smiling secretly. "You are entitled to an inside seat. Your fare has been paid."

"It's not been paid yet, Thaddeus," corrected Mrs. Quin nervously. "I haven't seen the driver to ask how much it would be."

As she spoke, Angel noticed that two of the passengers exchanged amused glances and he wondered why. He couldn't see anything funny about Mrs. Quin's remark.

Then suddenly, and without any warning, they were underway. There was the crack of a long whip in the air, and the coach lurched forward, jolting everyone onto his neighbor's lap. The next minute they were turned around and rattling over the rough boards of the wharf.

"Gracious me!" Mrs. Quin sat up and straightened her bonnet. "I didn't even know the driver had sneaked up to his seat."

"It was a surprise," admitted the professor. For a moment he stared through the window at the town, which they were already leaving behind. Then he turned to Angel, and his expression was one of forced severity.

"And now, my boy," he announced grandly. *"Tempus fugit,* and we must lose no golden opportunity. I have resolved to employ these hours while we are en route to El Dorado by beginning your instruction. Do you know the scales?"

Angel swallowed. He looked across at the five miners, all of whom were observing them with great interest.

"No, sir," he admitted feebly.

Chapter 5

"Shingle Springs! We rest the team twenty minutes here. You can stretch your legs, everybody that's a mind to!"

The Concord stage had come to a stop. For what had seemed like hours, the passengers had been bumped and jostled together unmercifully. Even the padded seats were no help, not when you were being jabbed by your neighbor's sharp elbow or found yourself perched atop his bony knees.

They had been traveling as fast as the wind—ten miles an hour, one of the passengers insisted—over a road that in places had been hacked through tall stands of timber and was cluttered with rocks and potholes. Now the driver had pulled his sweating horses to a halt, climbed down from his high seat, and opened the coach door.

Angel did not need a second invitation. He was the

first one out. He stood off at a little distance, observing the others out of the corner of his eye.

The first singing lesson had been a humiliating experience. It had not lasted long, for the professor soon had decided that scales were impossible when the singer's breath was being knocked out of him by bumps.

The passengers were sorry to have it come to an end. They had regarded the whole thing as a comedy performed for their amusement and had laughed from start to finish. Professor Quin had ignored them completely, even when they called out suggestions and comments, but Angel had been so embarrassed that he had considered opening the door and jumping out of the stage. Even after the professor had brought the lesson to an end, he could not make himself look across at the miners on the opposite seat.

"Time to find out where we're going," called the driver jovially. He was a tall, broad-shouldered man who wore a jacket made of Indian-tanned leather, and, around his neck, a knotted handkerchief, which could be pulled up over his nose when the dust became too thick. "Let's have your stops between here and Hangtown."

Several of the miners were going to Hangtown itself, one to a place called Rescue and another to a curiously named camp called Pinch-em-tight. When they heard this, those destined for Hangtown groaned.

"That's clean off the road, Hank," one of them protested. "It takes us a couple of hours, maybe three, out of the way. And you'll make us pay for it."

"You get the benefit of the extra ride, don't you?" pointed out the driver reasonably. "Why shouldn't you pay?" He turned to the professor. "Where you and your party headed, mister?"

"To the Mother Lode. The exact center, called, I believe, Mokelumne Hill," Professor Quin told him proudly.

"What is the fare?" asked Mrs. Quin breathlessly. "I wish to know that before we start."

"You already started, ma'am," the driver reminded her in a surprised tone. "And I can't tell you the fare till I know where all we're going. The boys up top ain't told me their stops yet."

"You see, ma'am," explained one of the miners kindly, "the fare's not always the same. If we went in a straight line from Sacramento to Hangtown, say, the fare'd be such and such. But already we're making two detours to let off passengers, and since it's a longer ride it'll cost us more."

"But that's unfair," gasped Mrs. Quin. "It's dishonest."

"There's only one stage line. If you're going to ride it, they got you over a barrel, ma'am."

"How far is it from this—this Hangtown," she gave a little frown of disapproval, "to Mok—wherever it is we're going?"

The miner pulled his chin thoughtfully.

"Quite a piece, ma'am," he admitted cautiously. "Hangtown's a little out of the way, and you'll have to swing back a mite south and then go east a spell. If you'd gone horseback or by shanks' mule, you wouldn't have hit Hangtown at all. You'd take a trail up past Michigan Bar and on to Drytown, and then east."

"Then we shouldn't even be on this stage," cried Mrs. Quin indignantly. "Thaddeus, we've been cheated."

59

"No, ma'am," corrected the man quickly. "I said by horseback or shanks' mule. There's no stage that way as yet. If you want to go by stage you got to go this way, all around Robin Hood's barn."

"There, Almira. You see." For a moment Professor Quin had looked a little worried himself, but now he brightened. "While we are stopped, let us inspect this place. We might find nuggets."

Angel saw that the professor was starting in his own direction so he turned and walked away. He wasn't going to run the danger of another exercise in scales.

Shingle Springs was not a large camp. It consisted of a few shacks, one of which carried a roughly painted sign reading "Store," but it did boast one brick building, which seemed to house a mill. Some of the passengers had made straight for that, and Angel could see that they were kneeling down and seemed to be drinking from their cupped hands. Obviously there was a spring of water, and he suddenly realized that he was very thirsty.

He walked in the direction of the mill as slowly as he could, hoping the men would leave before he arrived. At least two of them had been passengers inside the coach and had witnessed that shameful ordeal of the music lesson.

Unfortunately, the men seemed to be in no hurry to leave the spring. When they finished drinking, they stood up and remained there, talking.

Angel hesitated. He kicked at a clump of dry grass, and then bent over to inspect the damage carefully. The more he thought about it, the thirstier he grew. By now his throat had become so dry he could scarcely swallow. He had to have a drink! What difference did it make if the men did start laughing again, he asked himself. After he found Joaquin and became a bandit, they'd laugh out of the other side of their mouths.

He continued on to the spring, averting his eyes from the little group and trying to pretend they weren't there. He dropped to his knees and bent over the spring.

"Hold on there, boy!" protested one of the miners.

Angel's head came up with a guilty jerk, his wet chin dripping water over the new red shirt. To his relief, the man wasn't laughing. He was serious; his face showed concern.

"That ain't no way to drink, boy. Ain't safe. Somebody could come up behind and take you 'fore you even knowed they was there. Dip the water up and drink out of your hand."

"Come on, Charley, you old Injun fighter," laughed another miner. "You don't have to be that careful around here. These California Diggers is scared of their own shadows."

"'Tain't Injuns I'm thinking of, Dave," said Charley in a reproachful tone. "It's them gol durned bandits, Joaquin and his ilk. Way I hear it, they'd sooner slit your throat than look at you. And what likelier place to do it than when you was leaning over a stream with your neck stretched out."

"I don't figure Joaquin or any other bandit would waste his time on a young 'un with flat pockets, Charley," objected the third miner. He was young, with twinkling blue eyes in a freckled face beneath a shock of unruly red hair. He was one of the inside passengers, and Angel glanced at him resentfully, remembering that he had laughed the loudest of all.

"That there Three-Finger Jack feller don't even care about how empty a pocket is," insisted Charley earnestly. "Way I hear it, he just kills for the fun of it. They say he's worse than Joaquin, for all he's only second in command. You mind what I tell you, boy," he ordered Angel sternly. "You drink setting up, and don't be sticking your neck out for Three-Finger Jack's knife."

"Yes, sir," agreed Angel meekly, but the humiliation of the singing lesson faded in a little prickle of excitement. The way they talked, Joaquin might be closer than he had imagined. He might even be around here!

His arrival at the spring must have broken up the conversation, for the men began drifting back toward the stage. Now only one of them remained, but to Angel's discomfort it was the red-haired miner. He had taken a bone-handled knife from a leather sheath that hung from his belt and was whittling on one of the small pieces of wood that littered the ground.

"What's your name, boy?"

"Angel." He permitted himself a quick glance at the moving knife. It would be a useful thing to have. He and Pierre had often discussed how fine it would be to own a knife, but such things were never displayed in easy reach. Expensive items like knives and guns were kept in the dusty interiors of shops.

"Mine's Kirk. Folks call me Red. I reckon you can guess why." He laughed expectantly, but when Angel made no reply, he continued, "You mustn't take offense that we laughed when your pa was trying to get you to sing. We just couldn't help ourselves. It's hard enough to talk, let alone sing, when Hank gets that coach to rolling good."

"He's not my father," Angel told him curtly.

The leather sheath hung on the left side of the man's belt, he observed, and it looked as though the knife might be a snug fit.

"That so?" Red did not seem surprised. "What you doing with him then, Angel?"

"They're taking me with them to the gold fields," Angel explained. For the first time he smiled. It was going to require skill and more than a moment to inch the knife from its leather casing. He must simulate friendship. "Professor Quin is my *patrón*. He will teach me to be a great singer at the same time that he finds more gold to add to his purse."

"Hmm." Red tossed the half-whittled stick onto the ground and slipped the knife back into its sheath. "A singing master, eh? Once when I was a little tyke back home, we had a singing master come to our town, and he set great store by them do-re-mi's, too. But he didn't last long. Folks wanted songs with respectable words to sing. First thing he knew nobody was coming round no more. He had to move on or starve. Never did hear how he made out. You say this professor is well fixed?"

"He's very rich," agreed Angel fervently.

"That's good," approved Red, nodding his shaggy head. "Because he won't get many customers for his do-re-mi's at Mok Hill."

"You know this place where we are going?" Since Red Kirk seemed about to return to the stage, Angel fell in beside him. He walked close on the miner's left, looking up into his face.

"Shucks, I live there! Know every gully and hill and rock and bush and creek thereabouts. Mok Hill's a great place, Angel. You'll like it."

In the roughness underfoot, Angel's ankle turned beneath him and he lurched against the miner.

"I thought you told the driver you were going to Hangtown," he said breathlessly, smiling his thanks as Kirk reached out to save him from falling.

"Might as well say that," the miner told him cheerfully. "We change stages there and pay up for this part of the ride. Hank's not concerned with what we do tomorrow."

They had reached the stagecoach by this time, and the passengers were climbing in once more.

"Where'd you go?" demanded Rowena reproachfully as Angel followed her up the step. "You missed seeing the man look for gold. He shoveled dirt in a pan and then dipped it in the creek and sloshed it up and down and up and down."

"And he did all that work for nothing," remembered Mrs. Quin dryly. "He said himself there wasn't any gold there."

"That's because he wasn't in the Mother Lode," insisted the professor.

Angel smiled politely as he took his place. His fingers pushed the bone-handled knife well down into the crack between the seat and the padded back of the upholstery. At least he would not join his friend Joaquin empty-handed.

Now the route passed through the wildest country Angel had ever seen. It seemed to be composed of one mountain after another.

"These are just little foothills," explained Red Kirk to the Quins. "They'll get steeper than this where you're going."

Since he had discovered that the professor and his family were bound for Mokelumne Hill, the redheaded miner had struck up an acquaintance. Mrs. Quin was politely reserved, but her husband was delighted and began plying him with questions.

Angel did not bother to listen. Despite the jolting and the bumps, he could hardly keep his eyes open. Last night's mosquitoes had shortened his usual sleep. He opened his eyes when they arrived at one of the camps to discharge a passenger, but after the first two stops he didn't even bother to do that. The little mining camps were all alike, a huddling collection of cabins and tents in a ravine between two slopes, with a line of dirty, bewhiskered men bent over sluice boxes or pans beside a running stream.

Once the professor shook him awake to answer a question.

"Angel, Mr. Kirk here has mislaid his knife. He recalls having it out at Shingle Springs. Do you remember noticing what he did with it?"

Angel felt the perspiration break out all over his body, and he darted a quick look through the coach window. They were climbing a steep grade. Below, the side of the mountain dropped fifty jagged feet of boulders and scrub bush to a stream below.

"You scared the boy out of his wits, Thaddeus, waking him from a sound sleep by shouting in his ear." For once Mrs. Quin was the compassionate member of the family. She leaned over her husband. "Angel, do you remember at our first stop this morning seeing Mr. Kirk whittling at a stick?"

"Yes, ma'am," agreed Angel, settling back against the seat.

"You recollect what he did with the knife when he was through?"

Angel shook his head. It was going to be all right. They didn't know.

"I guess he must have put it back, wherever he carried it," he said vaguely.

"That's what I thought." Red's voice was puzzled as

his fingers fumbled with the empty sheath. "I always do. It gets to be a habit. But it's not there now."

"It must have slipped out," suggested Rowena helpfully. "And you didn't notice."

"Hard to see how that could come about. It was a tight fit. Hate to lose that knife. I set great store by it," said Red Kirk thoughtfully.

Angel closed his eyes once more. After a few minutes he was asleep.

It was early evening by the time they arrived at Hangtown. This was larger than the other camps they had passed through and was built in a ravine surrounded by hills.

Red Kirk explained that in the beginning, prospectors had believed that all gold was found in gullies, washed down from the slopes above by the rivers and streams. Now they had discovered that some of the richest deposits were found on the hillsides and mountaintops as well.

As they bounced along, he pointed out a few scattered shacks built on the rugged slopes where individuals had staked their claims, but the majority of miners preferred to live in the original town and walk back and forth from their diggings.

"Have to cart their dry dirt down to the river to wash it, anyhow," he finished, shrugging. "Might as well stay put on their last trip. They claim it's safer than living off all by yourself, though I never been bothered myself."

"Does the bandit Joaquin come here?" asked Angel.

"What do you know about bandits, Angel?" demanded Mrs. Quin.

"I reckon he heard a little talk about Joaquin back at Shingle Springs," remembered Red, laughing. "Don't you worry, boy. Joaquin won't come to the boarding-house where we'll spend the night. You'll be safe there."

The stagecoach bounced and clattered down the last descent and came to a rattling stop on a curving street. The horses stood quietly, sweat pouring from their heaving backs, as the driver jumped down and opened the door.

"I'll take your fares now," he announced. "Fares first, then you can claim your belongings."

"Oh," said Mrs. Quin weakly, clutching her handbag.

Angel reached behind him and slid the bone-handled knife out of the crack in the seat and up the sleeve of his new shirt. He would have to carry it that way, held against his arm, for the blue jeans were fitted in the fashion approved by the miners, tight enough to stay up without suspenders or belt. If he tried to hide the knife in his pocket, the bulge would give him away.

With audible relief, the miners seated opposite the Quins piled off first, each one stopping at the door to pay the driver his fare. Since Angel had been the last one in, he was the first of their party to get up. He stood up as the last broad-shouldered back filled the doorway. At that moment, one of the horses shied at a distraction in the street and lunged forward, jerking the coach enough so that Angel was thrown off balance. He made an effort to save himself, and in that instant the knife slipped from his sleeve.

"Watch yourself, my boy," warned Professor Quin.

Angel's fingers were already fumbling on the floor

when Rowena called out. She had leaned forward past her father and her sharp eyes had seen the thin object under the opposite seat.

"It's Mr. Kirk's knife!" she cried happily. "Look, Papa. It had slipped under the seat, and now Angel's found it. Oh, won't he be happy?" She raised her voice and called loudly. "Mr. Kirk! Your knife was right here all the time."

Chapter 6

The next morning they resumed their journey and found that the steep slopes that surrounded Hangtown were only the beginning of the foothills. Whenever the coach stopped and the dust cleared away, Angel could glimpse an even vaster mountain range beyond. These, he was sure, they would never be able to climb, unless they did it on foot. Even here the male passengers were forced to get out and help push the coach up the worst ascents.

The road followed an old mule trail that generally ran between the hills, but there were places where the team and the sweating, straining pushers had to toil up and up. At the top there was always a pause, while the men all hurried to take their seats. Then, with a jerk, the coach would begin a perilous descent, the driver yelling and swearing in his efforts to slow the breakneck speed. The terrified passengers were jolted from side to side and frequently thrown from the seat to the floor.

Angel was wide awake today. Even his itching insect bites had not been able to keep him from sleeping last night at the boardinghouse. The straw tick had made a comfortable bed, and his stomach had been pleasantly filled with hot supper.

Mrs. Quin had made her usual fuss about the cost of the meal, a dollar a plate just for plain stew, but the professor had insisted that he was tired of eating cold things from the lunch basket. In the end she had given in, as she always did, counting out the money from her black handbag, piece by piece.

Since Red Kirk had apparently attached himself to their party, Angel wished that he hadn't taken the bone-handled knife yesterday. Of course, a knife was a fine thing to have, and he had always wanted one, but he should have remembered that his new clothes provided no hiding place for stolen goods. He was bound to be found out. Even now he wasn't sure that the redheaded miner had accepted the explanation that the knife had slipped under the seat. Kirk hadn't said anything, but the look with which he had accepted the return of his property had been a little odd.

Today, however, the miner seemed to have put the incident from his mind. He was happy to be returning after a week's vacation in San Francisco, and was filled with stories about the countryside through which they were passing.

"We're coming into Drytown," he told them. "Likely we'll stop here to change horses. Soon as I get this far, I always feel like I was coming home, for it's only twelve miles more to Jackson, then a hip and a holler on to Mok Hill."

Drytown was perched on a shoulder of a steep hill, with a wooded crest rising up behind it. The road twisted upward around a bend so that it was impossible to see the whole town from any one point. The buildings on either side of the camp were reached by rough, wooden steps, with plank sidewalks running in front of them, but no one was using the walks. Except for a man who appeared at the livery stable when the stage drove up, the town looked empty.

"Where is everyone?" asked Professor Quin in surprise, as they climbed down to rest their legs.

"Down there." Red grinned and motioned with his head.

The hill continued on below the town, and a small stream ran at the bottom of the slope. Both sides of the bank were dotted with men bent over pans and sluice boxes. None had bothered to look up at the noisy arrival of the stagecoach.

"This is the Mother Lode?" Professor Quin leaned over a flimsy railing to peer into the ravine below.

"This is it," agreed Red, grinning widely.

"Then those men down there are gathering riches with either hand!" The professor turned, giving orders briskly. "Almira, Rowena, Angel! Look around you. Inspect every pebble underfoot."

"No need for that," Red told him good-naturedly. "No quartz to speak of around Drytown. But there's no place else so rich in dust, except maybe Murphy's or Hunt's Gulch. Why, most of them fellows down there's likely panning their two ounces every day, regular as clock work. And Drytown gold fetches $17.75 the ounce, too, not just $16, like in some places."

Professor Quin's lips moved silently as he multiplied to himself.

"But that's only $35.50 a day!" he protested.

"It's wonderful, Thaddeus," cried Mrs. Quin eagerly. "Let's tell the driver to take our trunks from the coach. Let's stay here."

"Nonsense." He resettled the tall hat more firmly on his head. "There are rich nuggets farther on. Why waste our time on dust?"

Red rubbed his scratchy chin and regarded the professor doubtfully.

"It's not that I wouldn't like your company clear to Mok Hill." His voice was troubled. "But it's only fair to warn you that a lot of them stories about folks picking up rocks made of solid gold have been considerable exaggerated. There's only one sure way of getting gold, and that's by using plenty of sweat."

"Thank you for your advice." Professor Quin smiled pleasantly, but his tone was one of disbelief. "Would you care to walk a bit, my dear?" He turned to his wife, offering his arm. "We seem to have the streets to ourselves."

With Mrs. Quin clinging to one side and Rowena to the other, they began carefully picking their way down the loose planking that formed the sidewalk. Angel stayed behind. As far as he could see, the town consisted largely of saloons, and he found it far more interesting to watch the stableman fit the fresh team of horses into the harness of the coach.

"I'm fearful the professor's in for a shock." Red Kirk

shook his shaggy head. "I seen fellows like that before, and you might as well save your breath. But I feel real sorry for that nice little wife of his."

"Her?" Angel looked at him in amazement. How could anyone waste pity on an old skinflint like Mrs. Quin?

"Yes, her." Red grinned down at him, but did not bother to give his reasons.

A second man, whom they had not seen before, crossed the street to the stage. He carried a metal box, which must have been heavy for it took both hands to hold it.

"This goes to the mint at Mount Orphir," he told the driver, surrendering his burden with obvious relief.

"Another shipment?" The driver seemed surprised. He mounted the step and stowed the box on the floor under his feet. "They're taking it out pretty fast."

"Will MacBee and John Stephens both hit it lucky," explained the man. "Run into rich crevices, both of them. The rest's just the usual."

Angel's brain began to work rapidly. He knew what the heavy box contained. There had been enough clues in the brief conversation to tell him that the stage would be carrying gold dust. He looked up and saw Red Kirk watching him.

"Gives you something to think about, don't it?" asked Red, smiling. "You might say it's kind of a responsibility, too."

"What is?"

"Why, the agent putting all that trust in us that way. You don't think for a minute he'd have handed over that dust if he hadn't known you and me was honest men?"

Angel made himself smile politely, but he decided he would have to amend his opinion of the big miner. Red

Kirk wasn't very smart or he would have known that thieves and pickpockets always tried to give the appearance of being honest citizens.

"Only two people was supposed to know that this stage would be carrying gold," continued Red carefully. "The agent and the driver. Now they trusted us with the secret, too. I figure we should take that as a compliment."

"Won't they tell the other passengers?"

"No, and you mustn't either," cautioned Red. "It might worry them some to know we had all that dust aboard. Mrs. Quin especially. Sometimes news leaks out about a certain stage carrying gold. Then it gets held up."

Joaquin! thought Angel quickly. Maybe his friend Joaquin would learn about their stage, and he'd see him this very day. He looked down to hide his excitement.

The fresh team was finally in place, and the driver shouted to his scattered passengers. For the first time Angel noticed the round length of metal extending slightly over the edge of the high seat.

"The driver has a gun," he whispered to Red.

"Hope he won't need it," said the miner softly. "Hush up about it now."

Angel was very quiet as they started off once more. His mind was busy with the contents of that heavy box beneath the driver's seat. He wished that he had asked its value. It must be a lot, for the box had seemed heavy. From time to time he looked at Red on the opposite seat and they exchanged knowing glances. He felt important to be entrusted with such a secret, but his thoughts kept returning to his friend Joaquin. Perhaps this was the day when they would be reunited.

Just over the next hill was a second mining camp very

similar to Drytown. It was called Amador City, Red told them, and the following town would be Jackson. The stage was scheduled to include detours to Bedbug and Pokersville, but these were being canceled. The passengers for those camps would have to continue on to Jackson. The driver made the announcement of this change as the passengers boarded. His tone had been brusque, and he had given no reason, but Angel and Red knew. He wanted to complete the run and get rid of his responsibility as soon as possible.

After leaving Amador City, they cut through a sizable stand of pine forest. Manzanita bushes grew thickly here, some as tall as the smaller jack pine, with heavily leafed branches that spread themselves like green curtains. The road was narrow, little more than a trail, and so filled with ruts that the driver was forced to slow his team to a walk. The passengers clung with both hands to the padded seats, trying to retain their balance.

Without warning, a shot sounded outside. The coach came to an abrupt, spine-jarring stop. Mrs. Quin screamed and Rowena began to cry. Angel looked quickly at Red before he pressed his nose against the window. Powdered dust coated the glass, and it was like trying to see through a yellow cloud.

"What is the meaning of this? Why are we stopping? Was that gunfire we heard?" demanded the professor.

"We're carrying gold," said Red briefly. "Somebody found out."

The next moment the coach door was opened from the outside and the dusty face of a Mexican looked in on them.

76

"Out, señores." He motioned significantly with a rifle, which he held carefully with both hands. "You also, señora, and the señorita too."

"This is an outrage," declared Professor Quin, but he lost no time following the miners from the coach.

There were a half-dozen mounted men who had ridden out from behind the concealing manzanita as the stage drew opposite. Two of them held extra horses with empty saddles. They wore the usual trappings of Mexican *vaqueros*, embroidered shirts, leather chaps, and wide-brimmed sombreros. Long, silver spurs glittered on the heels of their dusty boots. None was masked, and as Angel's eyes turned from one to another, his heart sank with disappointment. These were certainly Mexican bandits, but not the ones he sought. This was some small, inferior band. It did not belong to his friend Joaquin Murieta.

"Stand quite still. All in one place," called one of the horsemen as he prepared to dismount. "Do not make me nervous by moving. When I am nervous, my finger tugs the trigger of my gun. Sometimes I shoot somebody, as I did the driver of your coach."

Mrs. Quin screamed.

"The driver! He shot the driver!"

Angel glanced up at the high seat. The driver was crumpled in a heap, the reins had fallen from his hands. The sun glinted on the metal gun barrel still behind him. Obviously the attack had come too suddenly for him to slide the gun out.

Angel's eyes turned from the man who guarded them with his rifle to the Mexican who stood holding the stage's lead horses. Then he looked over at the mounted riders who sat calmly watching the whole proceeding. Every one of them was grinning.

He felt anger boil inside of him. There was nothing to smile about. Robbing a stage was one thing. It took daring and skill. But the senseless killing of an unsuspecting man was quite another matter. His Joaquin would never be associated with such a gang.

The last man to dismount was obviously the leader. He advanced toward them holding his rifle. Angel studied him carefully. He was tall and not too young, although no one could call him old either. Maybe forty. His brown face was seamed and weathered, and on one cheek was an old scar, probably from a knife, Angel decided shrewdly. His nose was large and sharp, like the beak of an eagle—no, like a vulture, he amended quickly —and his mouth was thin and cruel. Angel memorized each feature carefully.

"We'll take up a collection. Everyone must put something in my hat." With his free hand, the bandit removed his sombrero. "I will pass before you. Drop in whatever you have. Hold nothing back, or I may become nervous."

"You won't make much of a haul this trip," one of the miners told him boldly. "You got us on the wrong way, going in, not coming out."

"But then there would have been no gold box," objected the bandit playfully. "That is the important thing. But we do not turn up our noses at extra chicken feed. Turn out your pockets, señores, then pull out your shirts so I may look for money belts."

One by one, the passengers did as he ordered. There

was only a handful of coins in the upturned sombrero, but there were two gold watches, including Professor Quin's. When it came Mrs. Quin's turn, she handed over the black handbag tearfully.

"You're taking every cent we've got in the world," she told him. "What will we do? How will we get along?"

"Perhaps, señora, tomorrow you will make a strike." He seemed to think his answer very amusing, for he laughed uproariously.

Now that he had finished stripping the passengers of their valuables, the leader seemed to be in a hurry. He gave orders quickly in Spanish. The bandit who had opened the coach door, climbed up for the metal box of gold dust. The one who had held the team, loosened his grasp and struck one of the lead horses hard across its rump. The horse started ahead and the others moved with him, pulling the empty coach behind.

Angel watched the dust start up as the wheels began to roll, and he looked at Red Kirk helplessly.

"I didn't tell," he insisted wildly. "I didn't."

Red smiled and patted him on the shoulder.

"Of course you didn't. You and me can both be trusted, but somebody can't. Because they didn't have to guess about the dust being on this stage."

By now the bandits were remounted on their horses. They rode smartly out of the thicket, taking the opposite direction from the coach. As they passed by, some of them looked down and grinned at the little group standing alone in the sunshine. The leader was the last. He touched his horse with the silver spurs, making it rear, pawing the air with its front hoofs.

Then Angel's heart almost stopped beating, for before the horse and rider disappeared in the dust cloud, the man called out mockingly.

"*Yo soy* Joaquin! Remember Joaquin, *amigos.*"

Chapter 7

"We're almost home," announced Red Kirk gaily. He slid the frayed buggy whip from its holder to use as a pointer. "Yonder's Mok Hill. Straight ahead."

"Which one?" demanded Angel. He could see a great elevation of wooded ground, but it rose in giant bumps, hillock rising upon hillock.

"Why, all of them. Course some of them's got special names, like French Hill, but when you come right down to it, it's all Mokelumne Hill. Some folks might argue the point, but to my way of thinking Chili Gulch is part of Mok Hill too. Leastwise, the slope to it is."

"I feel so bad about putting you out, Mr. Kirk." Mrs. Quin leaned forward from the back seat to speak over his shoulder. "You and all those kind people from Jackson who rode out to rescue us yesterday and took us in for the night. I don't know how we'll ever repay you."

"With gold, madam. With gold," explained Professor

Quin. The rich voice was undeniably impatient. "Never fear, Thaddeus Joshua Quin pays his debts in full."

Angel glanced back at the professor sympathetically. Ever since yesterday's holdup Mrs. Quin had been apologizing to people. He was getting tired of it too.

The runaway team with the empty stage had been picked up by honest citizens who promptly guessed what had happened. A rescue party had been sent out, and the stranded passengers brought to Jackson, where they were taken in by hospitable families for the night.

Mrs. Quin had not shed any more tears over the loss of her money, but she had done nothing but apologize for her inability to pay her way.

The professor was just the opposite. He apologized for nothing. If anything, he accepted all that was done for him as his just due. He had agreed instantly when Red Kirk suggested that they continue on to Mokelumne Hill and stay as guests in his cabin until they got their feet under them again. Mrs. Quin had agreed, too, but with certain reservations.

"Only if you let me keep up the work, Mr. Kirk, cook and wash and clean up. I'd like to keep track of everything it costs for our food, too. Maybe someday we can pay you back."

Angel was not consulted, but he decided that the arrangement was as good as any. It would serve until he had decided what to do.

Yesterday's encounter with the bandits had upset all his plans. He had been so sure that the celebrated Joaquin Murieta was the man who had befriended him. The stories he had heard corresponded with his own memory of the man who had shared his tent on the night of the Hounds. The Mexicans on Telegraph Hill regarded Murieta as their personal hero. They claimed that only greedy, rich people were robbed, and even they weren't hurt, except through their pockets. The poor were left alone, save occasionally when their virtue was rewarded with a little gold.

Angel had seen the posters offering a sizable cash sum for the bandit's capture, but these had been issued by the law. He did not have dealings with the law. He sided with the Mexicans.

Since yesterday, everything had changed. The bandit who had killed the driver and robbed the coach had ridden away calling out that he was Joaquin. There could be no mistake. Every man knew his own name. It meant that Angel couldn't be a bandit after all. He didn't care to be associated with a killer.

He had been very quiet all the rest of the afternoon and evening. Even this morning when Red announced that he had rented a team and wagon to transport them to Mok Hill, Angel had little to say. He was pleased to be allowed to share the driver's seat with Red, and he had even pretended an interest in the wild country, the swift-moving river, the pine-scented forests, the craggy rocks, and the sun-drenched clearings. But all he could think of was the thin, cruel mouth, the hooked nose, and the seamed face of the man who had shattered his dream.

Behind them, Rowena uttered an excited yelp.

"A bear!" she cried. "He was standing right there by that bush, looking at us."

"Country's full of them," chuckled Red. "That's why you need a cabin up here. Try to get along with a tent, and the varmints claw their way in and clean you out of vittles."

"If I'd had a gun, I could have got that one. Right between the eyes," she boasted.

Angel turned in the seat. There was no need for words. His scornful smile said everything.

"I could too," Rowena insisted angrily. "Couldn't I, Mama? Couldn't I, Papa?"

"Very likely." Mrs. Quin's mouth straightened in a line of disapproval. "But it's not ladylike to go around shooting guns, Rowena. Besides, it's been a long time. I don't doubt but what you've forgotten how."

"Not so long," muttered Rowena. "Zeb let me use his gun just before we left. He says I'm a natural-born shot, and when my arms grow a little longer—"

"That will be enough," interrupted her mother sharply. "How many times have I told you to stay away from that dirty old mountain man? Leaving him behind is one good thing that came out of this crazy expedition, anyway."

"I can recall a few occasions when we were grateful for Zeb Grant's friendship, Almira," said the professor reprovingly. "Besides, I thought we agreed that mastering the art of firearms was a useful skill in this country."

"And so it is, but Rowena's already learned all she'll ever need to know," declared Mrs. Quin, frowning. "She's getting on to be a young lady."

"Quite." Her husband gave up the argument as of no importance. All morning his head had been turning from side to side as his eyes studied the countryside through which they were driving. Now he leaned back against the hard seat and pursed his lips thoughtfully.

84

"This is not exactly what I had anticipated," he admitted. "Last evening I had several conversations with various residents of the town of Jackson. They have convinced me that even in the Mother Lode, the procurement of a fortune may be a bit more difficult than I had been led to believe."

"Whoever you talked to, they must have had powerful arguments." Red's tone was one of respectful admiration. "Most folks have to learn that the hard way. But don't you worry, Professor," he added quickly. "I'll help you stake out a claim, and who knows? Maybe you'll be one of the lucky ones."

Perhaps the professor would have said more on the subject, but at that moment they drove out of the trees and into sight of a small settlement.

"There she is," cried Red proudly, and pulled on the reins as a signal for the team to stop. "The fastest growing town in the Mother Lode. Just feast your eyes on that, folks."

The town straddled a rolling crest of one of the many bumps of which the entire hill was composed. Angel could not be sure whether or not it was the highest bump, for the trees grew too thickly for him to see through. The natural clearing had been enlarged, and the felled trunks thriftily utilized for construction. As usual in this country, the streets were not laid out in straight lines, but meandered in curves and angles to give access to buildings, and because the miners had no time to waste in grading, they were composed of one rolling swell after another.

After a minute or two, Red clucked to the horses and,

as they continued on down the street, he announced the civic points of interest on either side.

"This is the Golden Eagle Hotel, and across from it is Schutz's brewery. Real convenient, for it saves cartage fees. Yonder's Meyer's store, the first one around these parts. He carries a fair line of goods, ma'am, and his prices ain't no higher than you'd expect."

There were gaps in Red's monologue, for out of consideration for Mrs. Quin and Rowena, he ignored all references to saloons and gambling houses.

"That's the new Leger Hotel. Almost as fancy as some you see in San Francisco, ain't it?" He waited for them to admire the two-story stone and brick structure with its wooden balconies, before he called their attention to the opposite side of the street where another stone building was under construction. "And this one's going to be a real humdinger. Three whole stories when it's done. It's the Odd Fellows' Hall, but Wells Fargo plans to take space on the ground floor."

"Where's the church?" asked Mrs. Quin after she had duly admired the half-finished building.

"Ain't built yet, ma'am, but the way I hear it there's talk that we'll have one soon." Then he added hastily, "But we've got a fine burying ground, and we made sure there wasn't any gold there before we staked it out. Wouldn't care to be caught short like they was over at Volcano. They found out that they'd put their burying ground right smack in the center of a rich vein. It was the preacher that sighted it at a burying, just as they was about to lower the box. Well, you can believe he called off the services, and there was a big shuffling of bodies into a new spot where they was certain there wasn't any gold."

Mrs. Quin sniffed. Red, sensing her displeasure, immediately changed the subject.

"Down there's the French bakery. Old Raud bakes for the Ingots up on French Hill, but he sells to the rest of us, too. He makes a fine loaf of bread."

"I shall be baking your bread from now on, Mr. Kirk," insisted Mrs. Quin quickly.

"Yes, ma'am," agreed Red. "Where the street turns is the town square. We hold our meetings there. And Sunday preachings," he remembered triumphantly. "Go left a piece, and you hit Chinatown. On beyond's French Hill and Mex Town. But we'll go right, because that's the way to my claim. It's on the slope below."

As they drove by, Angel could see that in the exact center of the town square one tree had been left standing. Its branches were chopped off so that it could serve as a flagpole. His sharp eyes stared curiously at the white knob perched on the very top, and suddenly he began to grin. Anyone who boasted of her skill in killing bears shouldn't be squeamish.

"Look, Rowena." He turned in the seat. "Look what's on top of the flagpole."

After a quick glance, she began to scream.

"A skull! Mama! Papa! There's a skull on the flagpole."

"Really, Angel," sputtered Mrs. Quin angrily. "Really, Mr. Kirk!"

Above his dusty collar, Red's neck flushed warmly, and he slapped the reins against the horses' backs.

"It don't mean nothing, ma'am. Just a little advertising.

This is Calaveras county, and *calavera* means skull. But it ain't human. Not white human, that is. Just some old Digger Injun skull that was laying around."

Momentarily, Professor Quin came out of the deep concentration that surrounded him.

"'Alas, poor Yorick!—I knew him, Horatio,'" he exclaimed in ringing tones.

Rowena stopped screaming and began to smile.

"That's Shakespeare, Mama," she interpreted proudly. "Papa's saying Shakespeare."

There was no road leading to Red's cabin, and they would have to travel the last stage on foot, he told them regretfully. They left the team at the combination livery stable and blacksmith shop and followed a rough trail through the woods, the two men carrying one of the Quins' trunks between them. The second trunk had to be left behind for later transportation.

Angel had never been in a place like this before. It made him feel strange. Both Valparaiso and San Francisco were close to the sea. He was accustomed to air that was damp and smelled of tidal flats and fish, and to wind that blew gritty sand and carried the raucous voices of gulls. Here the air was dry and hot, even when he was in the shadow of a tree, and his new red shirt was soaked with perspiration. The smells were warm, too, spicy pine and manzanita and wild flowers whose names were as alien to him as those of the birds that seemed to trill and chirp in high soprano from every thicket. The path clung to the side of the slope, and from below he could hear water splashing over rocks, but it was the small sound of a creek, not the familiar rumble of a mighty ocean.

Red's cabin sat all by itself. It was built of logs, notched at the corners, and it had an oversized granite chimney at one end. Behind it was a small shed, open at one side and half-filled with split lengths of firewood, while strung between two small trees was a length of light rope, which the miner proudly pointed out as his clothesline.

"It ain't much." Red's voice was a little regretful. "But a man living by himself don't need any more. I wasn't expecting female company."

"We are the intruders, Mr. Kirk," insisted Mrs. Quin quickly. "You're kind to share it with us."

Red unlocked the door, explaining that the precaution was necessary because Indians often broke into empty cabins. There was only a single room. It had a pounded-dirt floor, a couple of upturned logs which served as chairs, and a table made of rough boards. There were shelves attached to one wall to hold provisions and a few utensils, while the opposite wall supported Red's bunk. This had been built into the cabin itself, and consisted of two parallel logs running crosswise into the room for a distance of about three feet. Gunny sacks were nailed between them, forming a sort of hammock, and dried ferns were piled on top.

"That's a good fireplace, ma'am, if I do say so myself, as shouldn't." Red pointed across the room to a blackened pit, which almost filled the third wall. A great oak log topped the opening as a mantelpiece, while the mud hearth served as a repository for such unrelated items as a pair of boots, an iron kettle, an ax, a gold pan, a wadded-up mass of clothing, a few empty bottles, and a Dutch oven. "Really heats things up, and hardly smokes, even when the wind's in the west. Dries things out real fast, too. Some of the boys they have to put on wet duds the next morning to go back to work, but that fireplace never lets me down. Even my boots get dry as Saturday-night biscuits."

"We are putting you out." Mrs. Quin's eyes were taking quick inventory. "It's built for one person."

"Don't give it a second thought, ma'am," he assured her quickly. "You and Rowena can sleep in here. Us men will bed down in the shed."

Professor Quin had scarcely glanced at the cabin. He entered only as far as the threshold, and now he spoke a little peremptorily.

"I am impatient to see where they are discovering gold. Let us leave the household matters to the ladies, sir, and be off to the scene."

Red looked startled, and Angel knew that he was disappointed at the professor's lack of interest in his home. But Mrs. Quin seemed to take it as a matter of course.

"I'll need water." She removed her bonnet and placed it gingerly on the table. "And where's your broom, Mr. Kirk? And cleaning rags? And soap?"

"The broom's there, ma'am." It was a moment before he answered. Then he nodded toward a handful of dried brush attached to a stick of wood. "Soap's mighty scarce. We use sand for scouring, mostly. But I got a little in that tobacco can on the shelf. We get our water from the creek. Angel can fetch it while I take the professor to the diggings."

Mrs. Quin finally discovered the water bucket in the debris on the hearth, and handed it to Angel.

"Hurry back," she said a little grimly. "There's a lot to be done around here."

The little creek was not far from the cabin. Angel dipped the bucket, tilting it carefully so that the current would rush inside. The creek bed was strewn with pebbles and larger rocks, and as he squatted there, he inspected them carefully. In this land of plentiful gold, it was just possible that he could pick up a nugget. After a few moments he gave up. The rocks were all brown or white or gray.

When he returned to the cabin, everything movable had been carried outside. Kettles and pans, sacks and cans, and clothing were all spread in the sunshine by the open doorway. Rowena was taking the dried ferns from the gunny-sack bed and throwing them into the cavernous fireplace, while Mrs. Quin was sweeping down the log walls with Red's improvised broom.

"That's not enough water." She turned to frown at the half-filled bucket. "We'll need three or four times that much. Why didn't you fill it to the top?"

"The creek's not very deep. You can't dip the bucket in," explained Angel shortly.

"Pour that into something smaller. And when you go back, take something to dip with," she ordered. "Rowena, if you've finished with that chore, go with him and help carry. Fill up anything you can find. And don't loiter on the way. We're working for our board, remember, and I aim to give fair measure."

For a moment Angel considered telling Mrs. Quin that he did not want to carry any more water, that he intended to follow the men to the diggings farther along the creek. Then he remembered that for a little while

longer, he was dependent on these people. The country was strange and a little frightening. Until he learned his way around, he was afraid to strike out for himself. When Rowena began handing him empty kettles and pans, he accepted them without argument.

As soon as they started down the slope, she began one of those tiresome conversations that Angel had come to dread.

"Do you think you'll like it here?"

He shrugged. How could he tell? He had only just arrived.

"It's different than I expected, too," she admitted. "I don't know exactly what I did expect. Not so many mountains and trees, I guess. I thought maybe it would be flat, and in places it would sparkle with gold. These

woods are a little like Oregon. We saw that bear, you
know, and there are deer tracks here."

"How would you know?" He sneered openly.

"I've seen them. Lots of times. My friend Zeb Grant
knows all about things like that. He taught me."

"He's the one your mother doesn't like," remembered
Angel. "The one who taught you how to shoot a gun,"
he added tauntingly.

"Yes." She continued to smile, ignoring his bad manners. "Zeb had a little cabin not very far from our
place."

"I bet you really can't shoot a gun," scoffed Angel
enviously.

"Of course I can. If I had one, I'd show you."

He smiled in a superior manner.

"You're safe saying that now that the bandits took all your mother's money. She can't afford to buy you one."

"She couldn't have, anyway." Rowena shook her head soberly. "There was only enough left to hold us over a few days till Papa found some gold. She only had sixty-three dollars left."

"Sixty-three dollars!" repeated Angel. Although he knew little about money, he was sure that this was not a great deal. It would not go far, not when you paid for everything you used. "She must have had more than that. You were rich. You had the money for all that land," he remembered.

"Land's cheap," Rowena told him simply. "But everything else costs a lot. That's all we had left, and the bandits took that. That's why Papa has to find gold right away."

Chapter 8

Angel could hardly believe it. He had misjudged the Quins. They weren't rich at all. They never had been. His mind was so busy readjusting to this new idea that he scarcely realized how hard he worked that afternoon.

When he and Rowena returned to the cabin, Mrs. Quin assigned both of them jobs scouring pans, cleaning ashes from the fireplace, gathering new ferns to replace the old ones from the bunk, splitting kindling, carrying in a supply of wood, and replacing the pile of Red's possessions on freshly washed shelves. Angel went from one task to another as he was told, but all the while his mind was working busily. There was much to think about.

Why had Professor Quin befriended him on Portsmouth Square? He had claimed that it was to train Angel's voice, but there had been only one attempt, that unfortunate session at singing scales on the stagecoach.

Since then it was as though the professor had put the whole thing from his mind.

If Mrs. Quin, who obviously controlled the purse strings, was so short of money, why had she consented to share with a stranger? But even as he asked himself this, he knew the answer. The professor had wanted it, and she had given in to please her husband. If what Rowena said was true, she always gave in.

He stood up, balancing the kettle filled with cold ashes from the fireplace, and stared across the room at Mrs. Quin. She was sweeping the floor with the unwieldy broom, sprinkling it first with water to lay the dust.

"Put the ashes all in one heap, out of the wind, Angel." She glanced up and smiled at him briefly. It was a different kind of smile from those she had given him at first. Now it held the beginning of reluctant friendship. "I can use wood ashes to make soap, and it looks like I'll have to do it soon."

"Yes, ma'am," he agreed, and carried them outside.

It was hard to get over the feeling that she was rich. That reluctant parting with each dollar for meals and transportation and lodging was the way he had imagined rich people behaved. The rich were greedy. They kept what they had for themselves. Mamacita had said that Mr. Schmidt was rich, and he certainly grumbled whenever he had to spend any of his money. But Mrs. Quin's reluctance had been for another reason; she was trying to make hers go as far as possible.

He dumped the ashes carefully, brushing away the fine film of dust that rose and clung to the knees of his blue jeans. Now he felt guilty. If he'd only known, he could have helped her bargain the shopkeeper even lower.

Thirty-seven fifty was a lot of money to throw away on a stranger. He wouldn't have done it himself. And all those dollars for meals, and the extra fares on the boat and stagecoach! It was one thing to squeeze money from the pockets of the rich, quite another to accept from the poor.

When he returned for the last load of ashes, Mrs. Quin had them swept into a pan and was laying the wood for a fire.

"We're going to have scant supper," she said ruefully. "Mr. Kirk's low on supplies. There's flour, and I'll set some dough and soak some beans, but that takes time. Looks like we'll have boiled barley tonight."

"If I only had a gun, I'd shoot a deer," said Rowena sadly. "Remember back home, Mama, when Zeb used to bring us venison? Angel and I saw deer tracks leading down to the creek."

"Maybe I can find us something to eat," offered Angel, remembering the French bakery they had passed in the settlement.

"What could you find?" It was Rowena's turn to be scornful. "You don't have a gun either, even if you knew how to shoot it. And I don't think you do."

"I don't need a gun. But I've got to go by myself," he added craftily. "You can't come with me."

"Maybe he saw some berrybushes off the trail that the rest of us missed," decided Mrs. Quin. She smiled at Angel kindly. "Run along if you want to. We can finish up here. But first you go down to the creek and scrub yourself off. You're all over dirt and ashes from the fireplace."

The faint sympathy that he had begun to feel for Mrs.

Quin vanished in resentment. Drat the woman, anyway. She was obsessed with cleanliness. Several times each day she ordered him to wash himself, and Angel had no other choice than to obey. As soon as he found Joaquin —the good Joaquin—he would never wash again!

He knew better than to say anything, however, so he started down the trail to the creek. As soon as he was out of sight of the cabin he changed course and began making his way precariously along the face of the slope. It was rough going, for now there was no trail and he had to hold on to bushes and boulders to keep from sliding down to the bottom. But he wasn't going near that creek! This time he wasn't going to obey Mrs. Quin's instructions. He'd just have to wash again before supper anyway, and he might as well have something to clean up.

He crawled for what seemed like a long time, then when he was sure he had left the cabin safely behind he clawed his way back up the slope. At the top, he stood still, catching his breath and looking down at himself. He was really dirty now. His new boots were brown with dust, and the knees of his jeans were caked with earth from crawling along the slope. His hands were black, and probably his face was too. He felt warm and proud of himself. Even though Mrs. Quin didn't know, he had really put something over on her this time! The feeling stayed with him as he continued on toward the settlement.

The return trip to town was all uphill, but it was cooler than before. In places where the trees grew thickly, the shadows were already gathering, and Angel hurried as fast as he could. He did not want to be caught alone in the woods at night. Nor did he want the street to be filled with spectators who might remember a boy carrying a loaf of bread. He had no long coat with many convenient pockets today. Whatever he took would have to be transported in the open.

He was too inexperienced to know that miners worked from sunup until dark, so he gave thanks to his patron saint when he saw that the crooked streets were empty as before. He went straight to the small wooden building that Red had pointed out as the bakery, and pressed his nose against the window.

There were two rooms, with a connecting door which stood open, so that he could see into the back. Obviously the bread was baked in the second room, and the front was only for sales. The baker was ready for his day's customers, for two tables were heaped with long, crusty brown loaves that made Angel's mouth water just to look at them through the glass. He could see no one stirring inside, and again he said thank you to his saint. He was accustomed to shops without doors, but this one was not going to be a problem.

He lifted the latch carefully, but as he crept inside his heart began to thump. The opening of the door had set a small bell to ringing violently. The next moment, a man, enveloped in a huge white apron, came out of the second room.

Angel's first impulse was to turn and leave. Then he saw that the man moved with a bad limp. Anyone so lame could not overtake a running boy. All he had to do, once he made sure that the two of them were alone, was to snatch one of the loaves from the table and dash away.

99

"*Bonjour,*" said the man, smiling warmly. "Good day. Hello. I have not seen you before. *N'est-ce pas?*"

"*Non, Monsieur,*" said Angel. Remembering a few words of the French, which he had picked up from Pierre, he added slowly, "I am new here."

Immediately the man broke into a long tirade in his native tongue. His smile stretched even wider than before, and he waved his hands with pleased excitement. He spoke rapidly, one sentence following another, many of them containing words that Angel had never even heard.

"I am sorry," he said when the man paused, as if awaiting an answer to a question. "I only know a little French. I learned it from my friend. I could not understand you."

"It is I who am sorry," said the baker. He took a long breath, then began interpreting his own speech. "I said what a miracle to see a French boy here in this place. You have the look of one who could be French. That is why I was misled. We have many of my countrymen here. They come because they have won the lottery, you understand. The lottery in our country. In La Belle France. It gives the winners the money to travel here to find gold. They are all young men, but grown men. It is a long time since I have seen one who looks like the young boys at home."

He paused to study Angel's face, and Angel, with his ear cocked for sounds of someone else in the kitchen, stared back.

The baker was of medium height, but his shoulders were very wide and the arms beneath his rolled-up sleeves were hard with muscles. One leg was considerably shorter than the other, and the sole of one shoe was

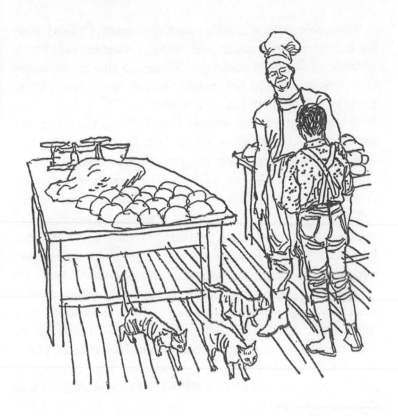

built up with a wooden piece to compensate for the difference. His black hair was peppered with gray, and his brown eyes had laugh wrinkles etched at both corners.

"I am Raud. Jules Raud." He bowed deeply as he introduced himself. "And you?"

Angel hesitated. This was not going as he had planned at all. He could hear no one moving about in the kitchen. Now was the time to snatch up the loaf of bread and run away. Somehow he found himself answering the baker's question instead.

"Angel. Angel Palma."

Why, this was stupid! It was the most foolish thing he had ever done in his life. Only Joaquin, the bandit, announced his own name at the scene of a robbery.

"I am enchanted to meet you, Angel," said Raud gravely. "And now I will tell you why it is that I am enchanted. For some weeks now I have been wishing that I could transport a young boy from home. A boy with two sound legs, not like this poor excuse of mine." He held out the shoe with the thick wooden sole so that Angel could see it better.

"What for?"

"To run the errands," explained Raud. "I bake the bread every day. Then Monsieur Leger must send someone from the hotel for his order. Sometimes there is no one to send, so he must come himself. He does not like that. My countrymen, who dig gold on French Hill, must come far out of their way for their bread. They must do this when they are tired from the work. It would be nice if Raud could save them the trip."

"You want to hire somebody to do that?" asked Angel in surprise.

"Why not? I must charge a lot for my bread. One dollar for each loaf. It is many times what it would bring at home, and sometimes I feel a little—how do you say it?—guilt."

"But you'd have to pay whoever delivered it."

"Naturally. That is why I wish for a boy. He would not expect the pay of a man." Raud's brown eyes looked at him sharply from beneath their thick brows. "Would you like this job? It would take perhaps two hours out of every day."

"Yes," accepted Angel quickly. He felt a strange

breathlessness, as though the little room, fragrant with the odors of fresh baking, had grown too warm. He had never had a job before in his life, except for the times when he sang with the band in the square. But he couldn't count that. Those were just occasions, entirely at the whim of Mr. Plumber, and the pay was in pennies and nickels. This was a regular job, a daily occurrence. He would receive wages! It was something he had never expected to have happen to him.

"Then it is possible that we can reach an agreement." Raud seemed to be speaking carefully, choosing his words. "You must first agree to a small detail—a change—"

Angel closed his lips together tightly, swallowing his disappointment. He might have known it was too good to be true.

"Whoever delivers my bread must be clean of person," declared Raud firmly. "His hands must be clean, and his face. A little dust upon the shoes is to be expected, but dirty hands—never!"

"I'll wash," promised Angel eagerly. "With soap! I'll show you how clean I will be. Is there some place here where I can clean up?"

"In there." The baker's black head nodded toward the back room and his brown eyes twinkled approval. "You will find a basin and water. See what you can do."

Never had Angel given his hands and face a more energetic scrubbing. His skin was tingling when he finally returned and held out his hands for the baker's smiling approval.

"I cannot pay much," warned Raud. "Say—twenty-five cents a day?"

"How much is that a week?" Angel frowned in concentration, and the baker mistook the frown for something else.

"That is one dollar and a half for six days," he answered quickly. "I do not bake on Sunday. But in addition, you will receive two loaves of bread free every week. At a dollar a loaf, that would make your wages three dollars and fifty cents."

"When do I start?" demanded Angel eagerly.

"Tomorrow," Raud told him. "Tonight, when my countrymen come for their bread, I will tell them that after this it will be delivered. Likewise, I will inform Monsieur Leger and the other regular customers. Be here at noon. The bread will be cooled and ready to deliver then."

"Yes, sir," Angel agreed happily. Then his smile faded. "Could I have one of the free loaves tonight?" he asked anxiously. "We just came today. There isn't very much to eat."

For a moment Raud seemed to hesitate.

"It is not usual to pay for a service in advance," he said cautiously. "You are sure you will return tomorrow? And the day after?"

"Oh, yes," promised Angel. "I'll work every day that you want me. I promise I won't let you down."

"Perhaps we could make the gentlemen's agreement," suggested Raud. "I will pay your weekly bread wages in advance, and you will promise to be here every day, or to send a replacement if you cannot come yourself."

When Angel nodded solemnly, he took two of the long loaves from the table and thrust them into the boy's arms.

"I trust you," he declared. "You have an honest face."

Raud was the second man who had told him his face

was honest, Angel remembered as he left the bakery and stepped out into the street. Red Kirk had said so, too, and they both spoke as though honesty was very important. He shoved the bread under his arm so that it was easier to carry. Well, maybe there was something to being honest, providing you didn't have to steal in order to survive.

Chapter 9

Red and the professor had already returned by the time Angel arrived at the cabin. They were standing by the small table, waiting for Mrs. Quin to dole out portions of boiled barley.

He put the two loaves down beside the barley pot and stood back, smiling proudly.

"Bread!" cried Rowena in amazement. "You never found that in the woods! Where'd you get it, Angel?"

"It's some of Old Raud's bake," recognized Red. He looked at Angel searchingly. "I never figured you had money, boy, and Raud never passes out no samples. How'd you come by it?"

"I earned it." Angel threw back his chest and stood as tall as he could. "At least, I'm going to. I got a job delivering bread. I work six days a week, and Raud's going to pay me twenty-five cents a day and two free loaves of bread every week. I got the bread in advance, because I promised I'd be there every day, or send somebody in my place."

"Why, Angel!" Mrs. Quin let the spoon slide into the barley. She reached out to pat him on the back. "Why, I think that's just about the finest thing I ever heard. Isn't it, Thaddeus? Isn't it, Mr. Kirk? Think of that. A ten-year-old boy with the gumption to go out and get himself a job before he's even been here a whole day."

"Two bits a day, eh?" Red threw back his head and laughed. "The old Frenchman's running true to form. He'll chase the legs off you. Clear up the hill where the Ingots live and back again."

"Ingots?" repeated Mrs. Quin suspiciously. "What's that?"

"It's what our French miners call themselves," explained Red. "Has something or other to do with gold, I reckon."

"The whole thing is quite out of the question," stated Professor Quin flatly. He picked up one of the tin plates of barley and tasted it. "Your time will be otherwise filled, Angel. Tomorrow morning I plan to begin your instruction. You must spend the remainder of each day in practice. A great singer, such as you will be, must devote long hours to perfecting his talent."

"But it's only two hours a day," protested Angel. "And we made an agreement." His eyes traveled between the two faces, one so sternly disapproving, the other wrinkled with laughter. He felt Mrs. Quin's arm tighten about his shoulder.

"You two galoots!" she sputtered angrily. "You should go and hide your heads in shame. This boy has done something fine. Something to be proud of. And one of

you tell him he can't do it, and the other pokes fun. I've never been so disgusted in my whole life."

She was like a small bantam hen rushing to defend one of her brood, and for a moment both men could only stare in amazement. Red Kirk recovered first.

"I'm sorry, ma'am," he apologized. "You see, Angel didn't say it was only two hours. Now that I come to think on it, that's pretty fair pay for a boy. And like I told you, Old Raud does turn out a good loaf of bread. It'll be real thankful tonight, having some to go down with our plain, boiled barley."

Mrs. Quin nodded an unsmiling acceptance of his apology. Then her snapping brown eyes turned to her husband.

"Well, Thaddeus?"

"Two hours out of every day is a long time," he insisted stubbornly. "Then we must add an extra hour, which will be required for going to and coming from this place of business. That makes three hours lost from his studies. It is necessary to think in terms of the end, Almira, not the present."

"But, Papa," pleaded Rowena, "couldn't he practice while he goes along?"

"Course he can," agreed Red enthusiastically. "It'll make the time pass quicker, too. There's nothing to stop him from singing and walking at the same time. Seems like I heard that them fellows in opera walk all over the stage, doing all manner of things, and they keep singing all the while they do it."

"Opera is the culmination of the art," pointed out the professor superiorly. "When they were engaged in study, its performers did not walk about and, as you suggest, do all manner of things. They concentrated."

"Then Angel'll have a head start on the others," argued Red. "For he'll learn how to do both at once."

"There's no need for you to think up more arguments, Thaddeus. It's all settled," declared Mrs. Quin firmly. "Angel's going to take the job that's been offered him. At least, there'll be one member of the family with a steady income."

Angel looked at her quickly. Did she expect him to turn over his weekly wages to her? Was that why she had taken his part? She was welcome to the bread, but the money was his. He intended to keep it.

"Very well." The professor conceded defeat, and promptly put the matter from his mind. "Why don't you slice some of that bread which Angel has so thoughtfully provided, Almira? Boiled barley, while no doubt nourishing, is not one of the most palatable dishes I have ever tasted."

Red Kirk awakened everyone long before daylight the next morning. He sat up in the darkness of the shed, yawning, and scratching himself noisily. Angel could hear him fumbling for his boots, which the miner had placed right side up "to catch the luck" on the ground beside him. This was followed by little grunts as he bent over to pull them on.

The professor came out of his sleep protesting. "It's the middle of the night, sir. The sun is not yet risen."

"It will be by the time we've got breakfast over and hied ourselves down to the diggings." Red's voice sounded jovial. He had told them last night that this was the day he was sure he would make a strike. He had a feeling in his bones about it.

Mrs. Quin and Rowena were still asleep, but at the pounding on the door, they arose and dressed hurriedly. Fresh wood, added to the banked fire, burst quickly into flame, and the black iron kettle was swung into place.

"There's only Angel's bread for breakfast," announced Mrs. Quin. "Though I was careful not to wash the old coffee grounds from the bottom of the pot, so I can add more water. I've got dry beans to soaking for tonight, and a sour-dough starter that's ready to use."

"Tomorrow's Sunday and the banks'll be open," Red told her. "After I turn in today's strike, you can buy whatever supplies you need."

"What if there isn't any strike?" asked Rowena.

"There's bound to be. That night we stayed in Jackson I dreamed about a hen setting on a nest of eggs," Red assured her seriously. "That means a pocketful of nuggets, sure as God made little green apples."

He could hardly wait to gulp down a cup of weak coffee and a large hunk of bread before he hurried away to his claim.

"Now, Thaddeus," said Mrs. Quin severely. "What about you? We're where you wanted to be. For two long years I've listened to nothing but the Mother Lode, and now we're standing on it. What do you plan to do about it?"

"Since I have not yet decided upon where to stake my claim, there is no hurry," replied her husband calmly. "Its location requires careful thought and full daylight. While I am awaiting that, I shall begin the boy's instruction in music."

Angel sighed. Only a few hours ago he had assured himself that the professor had completely forgotten about the music lessons. He hoped it wouldn't be more scales.

"Why don't you have your lesson outside?" suggested Mrs. Quin pointedly. "The fresh air might make Angel sing better. Besides, Rowena and I'll be working around in here, and we might disturb you."

The professor approved of the idea, and Mrs. Quin promptly slammed the door behind them as they left. Angel guessed that she didn't enjoy scales any more than he did.

As he stepped outside, he caught his breath in amazement. The rugged Sierras were black silhouettes against a pink sky, and close at hand the shadows still persisted. They concealed the woodshed behind the cabin and the trail leading down to the creek. He strained his eyes, trying to see through the darkness, and turned his head from side to side, listening. He had never heard such sounds before.

"What it is?" he whispered.

"Birds," said the professor in surprise. "Surely you've heard birds?"

Angel shook his head. The sounds came from every direction. Some were close at hand, and others were faint echoes from farther off. The birdcalls blended into a great chorus, so that it was almost impossible to pick out individual notes. They filled his ears with their music, and he found himself trembling a little from the beauty.

"They'll taper off in a few minutes," promised Professor Quin. "I'm afraid we'll have to wait, but we can start your breathing exercises. Every good singer must learn proper breathing."

Angel's responses to the instruction in breathing were automatic. He heard the professor's voice dimly, and he must have done as he was told, for there were no complaints. His whole attention was centered on the music of the thousands of birds who saluted the arrival of the sun. It was like nothing he had ever heard, and it made him feel small and insignificant.

Finally the great chorus died away. Only a few scattered voices persisted stubbornly, then they too fell silent.

"Now," said the professor briskly. "Let us get down to work. You will start by singing for me the lowest note in your scale."

Angel came out of what had seemed like a daze. He could only stare blankly.

"How low can you sing? Let me hear it. Don't strain. I want a good, clear tone."

Angel made two or three attempts before he reached a note that met with the professor's satisfaction.

"Excellent," he declared finally. "Now your highest note. No straining. No straining."

Again Angel did his best to please.

"Over two octaves!" The professor was delighted. "Wonderful. You have a true high soprano. Absolute pitch and clarity of tone. Now that we know your range, we shall proceed. You remember what I taught you on the stagecoach? Do, re, mi, fa, sol, la, ti, do?"

113

"Yes," admitted Angel miserably.

"Then sing it for me," encouraged the professor. "Adagio, if you please. Adagio signifies very slowly."

The exercise in scales continued until full daylight, at which time the professor brought the day's lesson to an end.

"That is enough supervised instruction for now, but you are to continue practicing. From time to time, short rest periods will be acceptable, for we do not want you to strain your voice. But practice is the important thing. And work on those pearlike tones. First shape them in your mind, then bring them forth."

Angel continued doggedly singing scales as long as he could see the black coat descending the trail. Then he permitted himself one of the short rest periods to ease his voice. As soon as he stopped, Rowena joined him outside.

"I'm glad you're here," she told him frankly. "Now I don't have to practice scales. Papa's too busy working on you."

"Did you have to?" he asked wearily.

"Oh, yes. But Papa says I haven't got much of a range. I'm like Mama. We can sing a tune, but that's about all."

Mrs. Quin came to the door carrying the water bucket and a dipper, which she held out to her daughter.

"Take them down to the creek, Rowena. Fill the bucket to the top."

"I'll go," offered Angel quickly. Any excuse to gain time from the hated scales was acceptable.

"No." Mrs. Quin shook her head. "Rowena can do it. You rest up for your job later on."

Rowena accepted the bucket a little reluctantly and left, while her mother leaned comfortably against the doorjamb.

"How do you like singing scales?" Her voice was a little diffident.

"I hate them." Angel was too unhappy to try to conceal his feelings. "When I get away from here, I'll never sing one again. Maybe I won't ever sing anything again," he added.

"I never could see much use to them myself, though I don't usually say so," confessed Mrs. Quin. "Thaddeus sets great store by them. I guess they come in handy in some songs, though. Did you ever hear one called 'Robin Adair?'"

He shook his head. The only songs he knew were those of the celebrating miners in San Francisco, and the few that he remembered from his earlier years in Valparaiso.

"My mother used to sing it to me. She came from Scotland, and I guess she learned it there," explained Mrs. Quin. She began to sing softly, and Angel listened.

"What's this dull town to me?
Robin's not here.
What was't I wished to see,
What wished to hear?
Where's all the joy and mirth,
That made this town a heaven on earth?
Oh they're all fled with thee,
Robin Adair."

Mrs. Quin did not sing very well, and Angel found himself wincing a little at some of her notes. Although he had never heard the song before, he knew instinctively what they should be. And it was as she said. He could hear little runs of the hateful scales in the melody, only now they had become more acceptable.

"I heard them! I heard the scales!" he told her eagerly when she finished. "Will you teach me the song?"

"I think I better," she said dryly. "If you know a song, you'll be practicing something. And I know very well that you'll close up like a tea canister if you don't know a proper song to sing."

When Rowena returned from the creek, she did not seem to find it strange that Angel was singing 'Robin Adair' instead of scales. She sat down on the ground and joined in.

"This is the way we used to do at home when I had to take lessons," she told him confidentially. "As soon as Papa left, we always sang real songs. Of course, it would be cheating if you didn't stop every once in a while and practice scales."

So Angel obligingly stopped every once in a while and ran up and down the two octaves that the professor had designated as his voice range, but most of the time was spent in singing songs. Mrs. Quin and Rowena knew a lot of them: 'The Last Rose of Summer,' 'The Blue Bells of Scotland,' 'By Cool Siloam's Shady Rill,' 'Gaily the Troubador,' and 'The Minstrel Boy.' Angel absorbed them one after another, and kept demanding more. At last Mrs. Quin shook her head.

"I've got no more voice left than a crow," she admitted. "And I can't remember when I've wasted a whole morning like this, either. I'd like to have spent it washing, but you can't wash without soap and there's none left. I've got wood ashes, but no grease to make it with."

"It's almost noon, anyway." Rowena squinted at the sun. "I'm getting hungry."

"It's time to go to the bakery." Angel jumped to his feet. He avoided Mrs. Quin's eyes as he added gruffly, "I guess I better wash up first though. Mr. Raud's errand boy has to be clean."

Raud was ready for him when he arrived. Two large baskets, filled with long loaves of freshly baked bread, stood waiting.

"After this you will go first to the hotel," he explained. "Today there was not time to notify Monsieur Leger. He has already sent for his order. Take these baskets to my compatriots on French Hill. If there is no one about, you will leave them on the table in the largest building, the one under the flagpole. You cannot miss it."

As he gave directions for reaching the place, Angel thought briefly of Red's comment last night. French Hill was no short jaunt from the little settlement of Mokelumne Hill. He would be walking his legs off. But it was a job, and it paid real wages, the first he had ever earned. He took up the baskets and started out blithely.

The trail led past the small colony where the Chinese

117

miners had congregated. They had not used native logs for their shacks, but had purchased lengths of rough lumber and paid to have it carted in. To save wood, the buildings were erected close together, each side wall doing double duty for two houses. This gave the appearance of one long, continuous structure, with a hard-beaten path running before it.

Angel followed the path, staring at the weathered fronts of the shacks. It must be very dark inside, he decided, for although there were occasional small windows, they were sealed off with what appeared to be thick greased paper. As he neared the end of the row, the last door opened wide enough to permit a small, bent figure to squeeze through.

Angel stopped, for the path was narrow and the man had stepped out directly in front of him.

The Chinese was dressed in the traditional garments of his countrymen, a dark-blue jacket above long pantaloons that reached to his wooden sandals. His hat was a cone of split bamboo that extended to his nose, and down his back hung a neatly braided pigtail. In one hand he carried a small stool, and as he bent to place it on the ground before his doorway, he caught sight of Angel. Immediately he cried out in surprise.

"Hello," said Angel uncertainly.

There was fear in the black eyes that stared up out of an incredibly wrinkled face. The man was very old. He must have come from his close, dark quarters to enjoy the warmth of the sunshine, and was startled at seeing a stranger. Angel made himself smile reassuringly.

"Hello," he repeated. "The sun feels good."

The Chinese straightened up, letting the stool fall

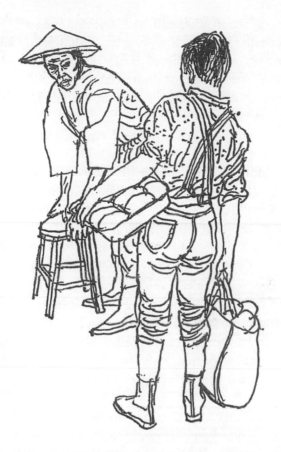

with a clatter against the ground. The black eyes were still frightened and filled with suspicion. Angel shrugged and stepped around him. Obviously the old man did not speak English.

French Hill was a great surprise. It was so tidy, so thoughtfully laid out. Its residents also had used lumber for their shacks, but each small building was separate, with a plot of ground around it and neat paths running between. In the very center was a tall pole from which fluttered the tricolor flag of France, and beneath it was the largest building of all, long and narrow, with a pointed roof.

No one was in sight, but Raud had already given instructions. Angel walked to the large building and boldly opened the door.

"Who is it?" called a voice from within. The words were in French.

"I've brought your bread. I work for Raud at the bakery." Angel made his explanation in English, for it was more than he could manage in French.

"Put it on the table, if you please," answered the man.

Unlike the Chinese, the French buildings had windows filled with glass, so Angel had no trouble seeing that the occupant of the room was sitting in a straight chair drawn up before a dying fire. He had wrapped himself in a heavy coat, with the collar turned up about his ears so that only the top of his black head protruded. His bare feet were soaking in a tub of water.

"You see before you one who suffers from the ague, from the chills and fever," explained the man petulantly. The words were muffled by the folds of the coat. "It comes from standing all day in rivers like melted ice. Since you are here, perhaps you would be so good as to throw more wood upon the fire."

Angel crossed the room, staring down curiously. Between the thick woolen folds, bright black eyes stared back at him.

"But first," remembered the Frenchman hastily, as Angel reached for one of the logs arranged in a neat pile by the hearth, "perhaps you will heat the water in which I soak my aching feet? It grows most cool."

Angel unhooked the black kettle hanging from a crane above the embers and poured the contents into the tub. The folds of the coat parted slightly as the hot water mixed with the cool, and beneath a sparse mustache, a red mouth smiled with pleasure.

"I see you have used the last of it," he observed. "On the shelf by the doorway you will find more water. If it is not too much trouble—"

Angel refilled the kettle and hung it back on the crane before he rebuilt the fire. He could feel the black eyes watching him carefully, observing every move. When he had finished, he brought one of Raud's loaves of bread from the table and held it out to the man.

"You might get hungry," he anticipated.

"You are my friend," declared the man earnestly. "And Louis Renald does not forget a friend. Your name?"

"Angel. Angel Palma." This time he said it loudly, secure in the knowledge that the Frenchman would not laugh. Pierre had never thought it a strange name.

When he started back down the hill, he finally recalled Professor Quin's instructions. He had forgotten that he was supposed to spend the time, going and coming, in practicing scales. He began at once, and since there was no one in sight, Angel dutifully ran up and down two octaves of do-re-mi's. But as soon as he reached the bottom of the slope and found himself on the main trail, he changed to 'Robin Adair' and the other songs he had learned that morning.

The old Chinese was still in front of his house,

but by now he had recovered sufficiently from his fright to sit on the stool. Angel saw him from a distance and stepped off the path to walk on the rough ground. He continued singing as he passed by and pretended not to notice the old man. He had experienced enough fear in his own life. He didn't want to cause it in another.

Just as he reached the edge of the settlement, he had to jump to one side of the road again. Rounding the corner, at the crossing of the silent street that led into town, came a horseman. He was riding fast. Dust spiraled up from beneath the pounding hoofs, rising and streaming out in a saffron cloud behind. Angel had barely time to reach the side before the horse and rider were even with him.

Muttering baleful threats, which he had learned from the San Francisco orphans and of which Mamacita would have strongly disapproved, he glared at the horse and rider. Then the words died in his throat.

There was only a second before the dust rose to swallow them, but that second had been enough. There was no mistaking the black, shoulder-length hair streaming below the rakish sombrero, the high-bridged nose, the tilt of the firm, brown chin above the leather strap. The rider was his benefactor of the night of the Hounds. He was Joaquin!

Chapter 10

Red Kirk's hopes of making his biggest strike came to nothing. He had the poorest day since settling at Mokelumne Hill.

"Not more than a half ounce of dust," he told them that evening. "And I worked my tail off and friz the marrow in my bones, besides."

"What about your dream?" remembered Rowena. "The one about the hen's nest filled with eggs?"

"Never knowed it to fail before," Red assured her solemnly. "Only way I can explain it is a whole day went by before I got to the diggings. If I'd worked yesterday, then's when I'd of had the strike."

"But you worked in the same spot, didn't you?" she persisted. "What difference did it make whether it was yesterday or today? The gold wasn't there."

"That'll do, Rowena," declared her mother, frowning. "How much would you say this will come to, Mr. Kirk?"

"It'll bring about seven dollars when the bank opens tomorrow." His face had grown a little pink under Rowena's questioning, and now he made a great to-do about turning his wet garments, which were spread out to dry before the fire.

"Seven dollars will buy something," she said cheerfully, patting the leather bag.

Mrs. Quin hadn't wanted to take Red's gold dust, but he had insisted on giving it to her immediately. Since it was Saturday night, he planned to go into town, and if he had it with him he'd be sure to spend it. When she heard that, she hadn't argued any more. She had slipped the bag into her apron pocket and inquired of her husband concerning his progress.

So far, Professor Quin had not decided on a claim. He had spent the day wandering around, watching others work and asking questions.

"One cannot hurry these things, Almira," he assured her in beautiful, resonant tones. "It is my understanding that public opinion is against a man filing on two claims simultaneously. One must be sure before he decides."

"You'd better make up your mind soon, Thaddeus," she said tartly. "We can't go on living off Mr. Kirk. It's not right."

Angel thrust his hand into the pocket of his jeans, and his fingers caressed the thin quarter that Raud had given him. At least she hadn't asked for his wages. He had worked hard to earn them. His legs ached from walking so far, and his throat was dry from so much singing. He couldn't remember when he had been as tired as this, too tired to go to town with Red and the professor that night, almost too tired to think about seeing his friend Joaquin again.

He thought about him the next morning, however. At breakfast Red was overflowing with local news, and one of the items was about a recent holdup staged by a bandit group whose leader had announced himself as Joaquin.

"Probably the same rascal that took off with our money." As she spoke, Mrs. Quin cut viciously into the loaf of bread she was slicing.

"Couldn't be," he objected. "This was down at Sonora, which is a far piece south from here. We was held up out of Amador City."

"But they had horses," remembered Rowena. "Horses run fast."

"Not that fast." Red grinned with delight. He had been waiting for someone to say just that. "Near as we can figure, both holdups was at the same identical time. Or very near to it. No, this just proves what some of us have suspicioned all along. There's more than one Joaquin."

"But which is Murieta?" Angel almost stopped breathing. "Which is the good one?"

"There's none of them good, Angel," Mrs. Quin told him, frowning. "How could there be? Bandits rob and murder honest folks. They're bad, all of them. Don't tell me you liked it when they held up the stagecoach?"

Angel shook his head. No, he hadn't liked that, particularly when the driver was killed. But the Joaquin he had come to idolize didn't kill people. Or only in self-defense. He had given up the idea of joining his former benefactor as a bandit. Now, perhaps, he wouldn't have to rearrange his plans after all.

"Time to get going. That is, if you don't want to be late for the preaching, ma'am." Red pushed back the log that had served as his seat at the table and stood up.

"Give me five minutes." Mrs. Quin began gathering up plates. "Water's already hot, and it won't take Ro-

126

wena and me longer than that to get the dishes out of the way."

All of them went to town that morning. The Quins planned to attend the church services, which would be held beneath the flagpole in the square. Red had gold to be exchanged for coins at the bank, and a list of supplies, carefully written out by Mrs. Quin, to purchase at the store. Angel didn't tell anyone his purpose, but he meant to look for Joaquin.

Careful inquiry yesterday of the baker, Raud, had resulted in a great deal of information. Raud had told him that the horse and rider, who had nearly run Angel down, were undoubtedly bound for the little colony known as Mex Town.

Mokelumne Hill's residents were composed of many races, and on the whole they got along well together, far better than in many mining camps. Only in their housing did they seem to cling together, the French on their hill, the Chinese in one tiny section, the few Mexicans in still another.

"There was once a large group of your own country-men here," volunteered Raud. "They lived in Chili Gulch. A bad man named Dr. Concha brought many peons—slaves—from Chile. He registered claims in their names, but he himself kept all the gold."

"Are they there now?"

"No. California does not have slaves. When the miners found out what the bad Dr. Concha was doing, there was a fight. A very bad fight. Men were killed on both sides. Dr. Concha and his slaves had to go. That was two years ago."

Angel was only momentarily interested. His motherland had grown dim in his mind. Sometimes it seemed that he had been here forever.

"And the Mexican miners?" He drew the conversation deliberately back to a subject that might throw some light on Joaquin.

"They are not miners. Not them." Raud laughed at the idea. "They will not pay the tax required for foreigners. The French, they pay when they are asked. The Chinese, always. But not the Mexican. He says he is no foreigner, and this land belongs to him. So it did until a few years ago, when the Americans took it from him. Some of the Mexicans do not give up. They will not pay, so they cannot mine for gold. They live as best they can. Sometimes they find work on one of the few old ranchos that still remain. Sometimes they deal monte or one of the card games. The bad ones become bandits."

Yesterday Angel had not given the matter of Mexican employment much thought. He had met one bandit named Joaquin, and he had not even considered that there might be two. Now, as he walked along behind Rowena's swaying pigtails, he could think of nothing else.

"Look!" She stopped suddenly on the trail, pointing to a clump of bushes that had been bent and broken. "A bear went through there. If I only had a gun, I could shoot it."

"What for? What'd the bear ever do to you?" demanded Angel, tearing his thoughts away from Joaquin.

"Nothing." She wrinkled her small nose. "But he could do a lot for us if I got him. Bear meat's good, unless it's been eating fish. And there's lots of fat, so Mama could make her soap and wouldn't have to spend gold dust for it. And the skin would make a good rug or a blanket."

"Even if you had a gun, I bet you couldn't hit a bear," scoffed Angel. "Usually, people who go around bragging how good they are, aren't good at all."

"I am, too," she insisted angrily. "Some day you'll see."

They met only one man on the trail that morning. He wore a ragged shirt above dirty pantaloons, which were stuffed into high, thick boots.

"Morning, Snuffy," hailed Red, when he saw him coming.

From under the brim of his tattered felt hat, unfriendly eyes in a whiskery face inspected each member of the party as they passed him, but the man did not return Red's greeting.

"That's Snuffy Ballard," explained the miner, as they continued on. "He's not what you'd call a sociable cuss. He lives alone and just works his claim. On Sunday he goes to town to turn in his dust, and skedaddles back home fast as he can get there. Folks say he's got more gold deposited to his account in Frisco than anybody here on Mok Hill."

"Is that so?" said the professor thoughtfully.

"He needs a bath," declared Rowena. "He smelled like an old buffalo skinner when he went by."

Angel glared at her swinging pigtails. Why were the Quins always so quick to criticize the way people smelled? Of course, he had to admit that Snuffy Ballard gave off an odor that wasn't exactly pleasant. But that was his own business.

Long before they arrived in sight of town, they could hear the noise of the crowd. On Sunday, hundreds of miners thronged the street, which only yesterday had been empty and deserted. The majority wore red shirts and blue overalls, but none was as new as Angel's. Some were almost concealed by patches of every size, color, and shape. Other miners wore loose trousers made of flour or grain sacking, held up by improvised rope suspenders, and some had rough pants of butternut or wore the threadbare remains of former business suits. Almost everyone wore a hat of some sort, rimless derbies, disreputable slouches, or Mexican sombreros, and the weathered faces beneath were shining with soap from their once-a-week shaves.

A long line was queued up before the bank, awaiting turns at the gold scales, and every business establishment was being well patronized. It was a little like Portsmouth Square, Angel decided, only there was no band.

Red steered his little party past the livery stable and Raud's bakery toward the town square. There, beneath the flagpole, waited a small group of miners and perhaps half a dozen women. Mrs. Quin's eyes brightened as she saw the ladies, and she retied her bonnet strings with careful fingers.

"You're coming to the preaching, Mr. Kirk?" she asked.

"No, ma'am," he told her promptly. "It's not my turn."

"Not your turn?"

"Well, you see, ma'am, we draw lots." He was embarrassed at his slip, but continued honestly. "Everybody takes a turn listening to the Sunday preaching, but we don't all go the same time."

"That's not Christian!" Mrs. Quin was scandalized. "To keep men away like that. Services should be open to everybody."

Beneath his freckles, Red's face was scarlet. He refused to meet her eyes, but his voice was doggedly determined.

"Anybody can go who's a mind to, ma'am," he admitted. "It's just that when it's your turn you got to go. Other times you can do as you see fit, and here at the diggings most of us find other things we need to do on our one day off."

"Well!" gasped Mrs. Quin, but Red had already turned and disappeared into the crowd.

By this time the ladies had seen them coming. They weighed Mrs. Quin's modest black gown and bonnet against the bright dresses of the fandango girls who worked in the gambling halls. Then all of them hurried forward to welcome the new arrivals.

Mrs. Quin smiled and smiled, the professor doffed his tall hat and bowed gallantly, his rich voice professing his great pleasure at the meeting, while Rowena bobbed polite curtsies down the line. Angel only nodded briefly when he heard his name called. He had no interest in these miners' wives. He wondered idly why their husbands hadn't left them home. Not one was pretty like the fandango girls. Their hands were red and knobby, like Mrs. Quin's, and their faces were lined and tired.

He looked up at the pole in the center of the square. The skull was still there, but he had to look hard to see it. Today it was overshadowed by the bright flag that fluttered in a light breeze, thirteen stripes of red and white, and a corner of blue studded with thirty-one stars.

Angel knew that the last star represented the new state of California. He remembered when it had been added last fall. What a gay time that had been. When the steamer "Oregon" had docked, and its passengers and crew had rushed ashore shouting the news, how excited everyone had been! There had been a formal ceremony in the square, unveiling the flag with its new white star, and for almost a week there was a carnival atmosphere in San Francisco. People went around with smiles on their faces, and there was one celebration after another. Someone had bought up the entire stock of firecrackers from Chinatown, and exploded them on the square. And there was free food, and even an occasional coin tossed to an orphan. It was a day he would always remember.

In the excitement of meeting new friends, the professor had released his arm, but now Mrs. Quin turned her still smiling face in his direction.

"Mrs. Waite says the two benches up front are for the ladies, Angel. Thaddeus wants to be there too, so he'll be handy for the singing. Most of the menfolk sit on the ground in back. You can have your choice."

"Yes, ma'am," he agreed thankfully. Now he could get away. He would be free to walk up and down the street, looking for Joaquin.

"Never fear but that I'll ask you about the sermon when we get home," she added pointly. "So be sure to listen."

"Yes, ma'am," repeated Angel dutifully, but he had no intention of obeying her instructions. He would stay only until she was seated and the services began. Then he would leave. He moved back to the outer fringe of the crowd, awaiting his opportunity.

In a few moments, the preacher took his stand below the flagpole and directly in front of the benches. He was a tall man with thin hair plastered close to his head, and a long face burned as red as any miner's. He wore a black suit, over a collarless white shirt, and heavy-soled boots designed for wading in rivers. He opened the services by announcing a hymn.

"We'll sing 'Rock of Ages,' and if you don't recollect all the words, I'd be obliged if you'd hum along."

"A thousand pardons, Reverend." Professor Quin's deep, resonant voice was in jarring contrast to the minister's reedy tones. "May I offer my services in lining off the hymn? I am most familiar with the proceedings, having performed this function regularly at home."

"I'd be most obliged to you," the minister accepted quickly. "Somebody to line off the words is what we've been missing most at our services."

The professor immediately stepped forward, facing the assemblage.

"Rock of Ages, cleft for me, Let me hide myself in Thee," he announced in ringing tones, after which he joined the congregation in singing the same phrase.

"When I rise to worlds unknown, and behold Thee on Thy throne," called out Professor Quin when they neared the end, and those words were sung like the first.

Phrase by phrase, he recited the verses, and the miners and their ladies obediently sang them.

While everyone else seemed to take it for granted, it was Angel's first experience in lining off a hymn, and he listened critically. He didn't like it. From what he could tell, the melody would have been pretty enough if it could be continued through to the end. Broken up in pieces, it didn't sound like much at all. He was quite relieved when they came to the end of the fourth verse.

This would have been a good time to leave, but he was a little curious about what would happen next, so he remained a little longer.

The hymn was followed by a lengthy prayer. Out of respect, the miners removed their hats, which they held in their hands. One of them had brought a rifle, and as he stood with bowed head, he placed it on the ground beside him. Angel was standing behind the man, and he stared hard at the rifle.

It made him think of Rowena. The next time she started boasting about her marksmanship, it would serve her right if Angel handed her a gun and told her to prove it. Once she had failed in front of everyone, there'd be no more talk about what a good shot she was. He moved a little closer to the man.

The prayer came to an end, and everyone sat down. Angel sat, too, his eyes still on the rifle. It lay on the ground beside its owner, not more than three feet in front of Angel's nose. He wondered how he could possibly get away with it. It would have to be carried in the open, for he had no way to hide it.

The minister cleared his throat and began to speak.

His subject was sin. There was a great deal of it, and it must be dealt with promptly. Sin was all around them, and as good Christians it was their duty to fight it with every breath in their bodies.

Angel did not pay much attention. He was too busy thinking about the rifle. Perhaps, when the services were over, its owner might forget it. Or perhaps he would carry it back to the crowded streets, where he might stand it up against the side of some building while he cut off a chew of tobacco or stopped to visit with a friend.

The reedy voice went on and on talking about sin, and suddenly Angel was aware of a few other sounds. They did not come from the street behind, where the voices of non-church-goers kept up a distracting ob-bligato. These sounds were closer at hand and came from in front of him. A moment later he recognized them for what they were. Several members of the congregation had fallen asleep and were snoring.

He stared carefully at the back of the miner directly in front of him. It was not nearly so erect as it had been. It slumped, and the head was tilted downward.

Angel inched forward. Now the barrel of the rifle was within reach of his fingers. He moved it cautiously, his eyes on the bent back. The man did not stir.

Slowly, carefully, he began pulling it toward him through the dust. The smooth barrel was hot from the sun, and it was a relief when his fingers finally touched wood. Apparently no one had noticed what he was doing.

The voice of the minister rasped on, exhorting his congregation to turn from sin, and those who were still awake, listened drowsily. Angel stood up, clutching the gun as closely to his side as possible, but as he turned to leave the minister's voice rose in an angry shout.

"Boy! You back there with that gun! Have the goodness to wait till the end of the preaching before you leave. Don't you be sneaking off to take potshots at some innocent bird. Sit down!"

His loud wrath broke the lethargy of the congregation. It even woke the sleepers. Heads jerked around to follow the minister's pointing finger.

For a moment Angel stood there, his legs refusing to do his bidding. Then a new voice cried out, close at hand.

"Hey you! Stop! Stop him! That boy's got my gun!"

With that, Angel began to run.

Chapter 11

His long training with the orphans came back to him now. Angel's only thought was to get away from the angry miner. On several occasions, he and Pierre had been detected by shopkeepers from whom they had stolen various items, and had been saved by taking to their heels. They were safe as soon as they had been swallowed up by the crowd. One ragged orphan looked very much like another, and it was a simple matter to hide their loot under a hollow step or a discarded molasses barrel and return for it later. In that case, if they were caught and searched, they could always claim innocence.

Now as he headed up the street, he realized there was no place to hide a rifle, and what was even worse, there were probably few boys in Mokelumne Hill. He had been the only one at the church services.

Behind him he could hear the shouts of the owner

of the rifle and the pounding of heavy boots on the ground. The footsteps were especially loud, more than could be expected from one pair of feet. The miner must have been joined by some of his friends.

Angel turned to look over his shoulder, and the next moment he was brought up short. He had run into a hard, unyielding body. Strong, muscular arms closed around him, holding him fast.

"What is this? Why do you run, boy?" The man who held him spoke in French.

"Why, it is Monsieur Raud's messenger," cried another voice. "The one who brought our bread yesterday."

Perhaps a couple of dozen Frenchmen had been marching, two by two, down the dusty trail that led from their settlement. They were smartly attired in their Sunday best, blue jackets with touches of gold braid, and spotless white breeches, which disappeared into shining black boots. In his terror, Angel had not seen them coming. He had run straight into the arms of the first in line.

"Let me go. Please," he begged frantically. But the firm grip was not loosened.

"Thanks, Frenchie." The miners had caught up with them now. Their sunburned faces were angry, and the owner of the rifle reached out and wrenched it from Angel's hand.

"What is this? What has he done?" asked the leader of the Frenchmen. His voice was puzzled, but he continued to hold fast to the boy.

"He's a thief. He tried to steal Gus's rifle. Sneaked it right from under his nose while the preacher was talking." The miner's tone made Angel cringe. "You know what we do to thieves around these parts."

"It is wicked to steal," agreed the Frenchman gravely. "But this one is a boy. You cannot hang him from a tree with your rope."

"A few lashes on his bare back might learn him a lesson," growled another miner angrily. "Or we could burn R on his cheek. R for Robber. That'd show him."

Angel began to shake. If only he could free himself of that hard arm.

"Who's boy is he?" demanded Gus, the owner of the rifle. "He looks furrin. Where'd he come from, anyhow?"

"He works for Monsieur Raud, the baker." Louis Renald, the young Frenchman whom Angel had met yesterday, pushed forward. "Let us take him there, monsieur. I think he is a good boy. He was most kind when he came to our camp. There is doubtless some mistake."

"He's got to be learned a lesson," insisted one of the miners, and the others growled their approval.

For a moment Angel considered telling them about the Quins. They had brought him here. The professor had assured Sam Brannan that he would assume full responsibility. Then he looked back across the square and saw that the services were continuing uninterrupted beneath the flagpole. Only a few miners had joined in the chase. Perhaps those in front could not even see what was going on. He realized suddenly that he didn't want the Quins to know he was a thief. In their own ways, they had all been kind to him.

139

If he could keep them from finding out the truth, he would.

There was some debate about what to do with the prisoner. The miners kept insisting that he must be punished, and the Frenchmen claimed, just as vigorously, that since Angel was a child, some adult with proper authority must be informed first.

The Frenchmen won the argument, possibly because they outnumbered the miners, and the whole party started out for the bakery.

Angel, walking between the French leader and the miner, Gus, wondered miserably what they would do to him. They had seemed to agree that he was too young to be hanged, but he didn't want to be whipped, and he didn't want to be branded, and he didn't want to lose his job with Raud. The last, he was sure, would be a certainty as soon as the baker discovered that his new employee was a thief. No one had any use for thieves, except other thieves. He felt very alone and scared.

Since the French Ingots had marched into town in formation, they used the road instead of the path at the edge. Now, as they continued on, they marched as before, the miners walking along at the side of their two straight lines. They had nearly reached the bakery when someone hailed them from the narrow walkway in front of the first of the buildings.

"Gus! Scotty! Hey, Henri! Where you all going with my boy?"

Red Kirk had finished with his business in town, and was headed toward the square. A burlap sack, holding Mrs. Quin's supplies, dangled over one shoulder, and his freckled face, shining from its Sunday shave, stared at them in amazement.

"This your boy, Red?" Gus stopped, and so did all the marchers. "He's a thief!"

"Hold on now." With long, swinging strides, Red joined them on the road. "That's a dangerous thing to say about anybody, Gus."

"He stole my rifle. Slid it right out from next to me while the preaching was going on," reported Gus angrily. "We didn't know who he was, and he wouldn't say, but he's got to be punished."

"That true, Angel?" Red looked at him carefully.

"Yes, sir." Angel made himself look into the blue eyes that demanded the truth. "I tried to steal it, but they caught me."

"He's got to be learned a lesson," repeated Gus stubbornly. "It's only right. You can't let a young 'un get away with stealing. What kind of a man'll he grow into if somebody don't take him in hand?"

"Why, Angel?" Red continued to stare at him. "Why'd you try to steal the rifle? What did you aim to do with it?"

"I wanted to have it there the next time Rowena bragged about how good she can shoot," explained Angel. He hung his head, and his voice was so small that Red had to bend over to hear. "She's always saying how good she is. About how she could shoot a bear and never miss. The next time she does, I thought I'd just pull out the gun and make her prove it."

"I see," agreed Red thoughtfully. He turned to explain to the others. "Rowena's a girl about Angel's age. She's staying at my place for a spell, too, along with

141

her folks. And I have noticed myself that she does take on some about being a deadeye shot. We got no gun to prove whether she is or ain't."

Some of the French Ingots began to smile at the explanation, but the other miners were still unconvinced.

"He tried to steal my gun," repeated Gus stubbornly. "He's got to be punished."

"He's going to be," promised Red. He held out one arm, and as the Frenchman loosened his grasp, Angel walked over and felt it close around him. "I've got me a good, stout razor strop back at the cabin. We'll go there now, and I'll use it on him. If you'd care to come along, any of you, you can watch."

"No," decided Gus after a moment. "I guess you can handle it, Red. But if I ever again hear—if he dares to—"

"He won't," promised Red quickly. "This is the last time."

No one else cared to accept the invitation either. The Frenchmen marched on to the Leger Hotel, where they would spend the afternoon playing lansquenet. The other miners reluctantly returned to the services beneath the flagpole, and Angel could hear them congratulating one another for having missed part of the tedious sermon. He turned to Red.

"What are we going to do now?" he asked uncertainly.

"Back to the cabin," Red told him shortly. "You heard me promise you a walloping. I make it a point to keep my word about things."

"Yes, sir," agreed Angel meekly, and fell in step beside the tall miner.

The whipping hurt. Red used the long strip of leather on which he sharpened the edge of his straight razor. Angel had to hold his lips tightly together to keep from crying, but that did not prevent the tears which filled his eyes. He did not resent it. Red had promised the miners, and he had to keep his word. Besides, it was nothing compared to the other punishments that had been mentioned.

When he was through, Red hung the strop back on the peg behind the cabin door.

"If I laid it on heavy, remember it was for double," he said pleasantly. "For the rifle, and for trying to filch my knife back on the stage. I guess you're paid up now."

"Yes, sir." Angel walked gingerly over to the water bucket and dipped himself a drink. With his back turned, he could wipe away the tears without Red knowing. After a moment he added, "I'm sorry about the knife. I didn't know then that you were going to be somebody I knew. I wouldn't steal from somebody I know. I'm not as bad as all that."

"Where'd you ever get that idea?" Red took out his knife and cut off a small piece from the square of tobacco he had bought along with Mrs. Quin's supplies. "That it's fine to steal from folks you don't know, but you don't take from them you do?"

"I guess nobody taught me." Angel frowned, trying to remember. "It's just the way it is."

"The professor says he picked you up in San Francisco," remembered Red thoughtfully. "He says he heard you singing, and just sort of brought you along. I never asked particulars, because, like you say, I didn't know we was going to be friends. But since we are, maybe it gives me the right to ask. Why don't you sit down and tell me about yourself, boy?"

Angel shook his head.

"I guess I won't sit down," he said significantly. "Maybe not till tomorrow."

"That's right." Red seemed surprised. "Since it's all over, I'd plumb forgot about it. Well, then, how about us taking a walk? I can't spit tobaccy in here no more. Mrs. Quin wouldn't like it. But you haven't seen my claim as yet, and we could talk on the way."

Angel nodded. He had been curious about the gold mining, but so far there had been no time to see how it was done.

Red stood up promptly, leading the way. Just outside the door, he paused to aim a long stream of brown juice at a yellow dandelion growing three feet away. Angel saw, with admiration, that it hit its mark without spilling any to either side.

He remembered that this man who had saved him from the wrath of the miners, who had taken in a group of strangers as his guests, who kept his word and did not hold grudges, had said that they were friends. Angel was suddenly proud. He wished that there was some way to let Red know how he felt.

Because Mokelumne Hill had proved unusually rich in gold, the claims were limited to twelve feet across. There were many claims staked out side by side close to the little stream which ran below the slope, each one marked by a curious contraption which Red called a cradle or a Long Tom.

The cradles were the smaller of the two and were made of short logs or empty molasses barrels. They really looked like cradles, too, Angel decided, for there was a handle to rock them back and forth. He knelt down and peered inside. A sheet of pierced iron separated the interior into two halves.

"You see, Angel," explained Red good-naturedly, "the

idea is to rock the gold loose. The water and gravel wash through the open end. That's called the tail. But the gold stays in."

"I thought you did it with a pan," remembered Angel, frowning.

"You start with a pan, but panning's too slow once you got a prospect. Like to try your hand?"

"You mean, I can rock the cradle?"

"Later. But if we're going to make a miner out of you, you better start from scratch." Red walked back up the bank where a small pile of tools had been carefully deposited. When he returned, he carried a flat, rusty pan.

"Now along here's my lines." With the toe of his boot, he carefully drew two, long, parallel scratches down to the water's edge. "You be careful to take your dirt from off my claim. Don't go so much as a foot over, for that belongs to somebody else. It'd be stealing."

"Yes, sir." Angel felt his face grow warm as Red pronounced the word "stealing." He wasn't going to try that again, not while his friend was around. Maybe he never would again. Although he wasn't sure that he was ready to go so far as that.

"Now you fill the pan with dirt and gravel, and then you wade out in the stream a ways," ordered Red. "I'll watch you from the bank and keep dry. Six days a week is plenty to soak up cold water."

Angel did as he was told. He considered taking off his boots, since they were still pretty new, but he didn't like to suggest it. Red seemed to think that wading in boots was proper.

The water was deeper than it looked, and very cold. It reached nearly to his knees, and gravel crunched beneath his soles at every step.

"Squat down," directed Red, who had seated himself comfortably on the bank. "Now lower your pan. Easy now. Not too deep. Hold it with one hand, and rub the dirt and gravel with your fingers."

"It's floating away," cried Angel in alarm.

"Raise the pan a little," Red advised. "Just let the water swish through. Gentle-like. Now you circle the pan, round and round. And keep working at that gravel with your fingers."

It wasn't easy. It took some time before Angel mastered the technique. He wished that Red would wade out and show him instead of just calling instructions. But Red was determined to enjoy his day off. He said that a man who worked in the diggings six days a week could last two years, but that one who worked seven days was worn out in six months. That's why the mines were deserted on Sundays.

"I think the dirt's about gone," called Angel finally. "Most of it, anyway."

"Bring it in," ordered Red. "Careful now. Don't spill what's left in the bottom."

Dripping little rivulets, Angel sloshed carefully to shore. There was still water in the pan and a little gravel, but there were also some yellow specks. He held it out proudly.

"How's your sit-down feel?" demanded Red, as he reached up for the pan.

"It—it doesn't burn any more." Angel was surprised. He had almost forgotten about it.

"I reckoned that would happen." Red's finger prodded about in the pan. "Now this here is what you call a good prospect, or a strike. See all them little specks and chips? If there was only a showing, we'd say you'd struck color. But with a good prospect like this, you can figure it's safe to file a claim and build yourself a cradle, providing there's just one of you. If there's three of you teamed up now—one to shovel in dirt, and one to pour on water, and one to rock, then you go to a Long Tom. It's the same as a cradle, only bigger."

"Let's build one," cried Angel enthusiastically. "There's

you and me and the professor. We could all work to-gether."

"Which one of them jobs do you figure the professor'd be willing to take on?" asked Red dryly. "And keep at it regular?"

Angel shook his head. Somehow he couldn't see Professor Quin undertaking any of those things.

"But there's still me," he pointed out. "I should think two could work a cradle better than one."

"They could. Maybe they could even handle a Long Tom if they was spry about it." Red was scooping up the flakes of gold in the bottom of the pan. "But you've already taken on one job with Raud. And the way I hear it, the professor brought you along to give you singing lessons. Long as he still wants to do that, you're duty bound to hold your time free for him. You made a bargain, and you got to keep your word."

Angel nodded unhappily. He wished that Red weren't quite so insistent on people keeping their word. There were limits to everything.

"Here you are, son." Red had pinched up the gold flecks in the pan, and now he held them out. "You panned them. They're yours."

"No." Angel put his hands behind his back. "It was off your claim. I was just practicing."

Red did not argue. He grinned good-naturedly, and dropped the gold into his leather poke.

"Now that you're able to sit down," he said, "you can tell me about yourself."

Angel obediently sat on the bank. He began diffidently, but before he knew it his whole story came spilling out. He found himself telling things that he had never told anyone before, about Mamacita and Mr. Schmidt, about Pierre and the other orphans, and how they slept on the ships and stole their daily food. He even told about Joaquin, and about how he had planned to join him and become a bandit.

Red chewed tobacco and spit streams of juice with remarkable accuracy while he listened. He did not interrupt, even to ask questions or make comments. But Angel knew that he was interested, and that his own confidences would not be repeated.

When he had finished, Red nodded solemnly.

"Well, I reckon that explains a lot. If I'd a been

in your place, I'd a probably stole things, too. But that's all behind you, son. You don't have to steal no more, and you won't. I'd lay my last ounce of dust on that. You find yourself wanting something bad enough to steal, you tell me instead. I'll get it for you if I can, providing it's good for you. That's what friends are for."

"I will," promised Angel happily. "Only there's nothing I really want. That gun for Rowena was a silly idea, anyway."

"The Quins!" remembered Red, getting hastily to his feet. "They'll be long back from the preaching by now. And you'll be in for considerable jawing, having took off like you did."

"I know," agreed Angel. He wished they didn't have to go back. He wished he and Red could just sit here by the stream and talk.

"By the way," said Red, in an offhand tone. "Providing the Quins don't already know about that rifle, let's you and me keep it a secret betwixt ourselves. No sense in stirring things up when it's all over."

Chapter 12

To Angel's relief, the congregation sitting in front at the church services had been unable to see over the heads of those behind them. The Quins had no idea that the boy with the rifle who had been challenged by the minister was their protégé. Since Angel owned no rifle, they assumed it was someone else. They had other things to think about, anyway.

After his great success in lining off hymns, the professor had been invited to organize a choir. And Mrs. Quin, who had mentioned casually to one of the ladies that she intended to make laundry soap, had found herself besieged with customers from among the miners.

"Just think! They'll pay me twelve dollars for washing eight pieces," she exclaimed in wonder. "At that rate, I can pay all four of our shares of the board bill every week, with a little left over. It was galling to have to take so much from Mr. Kirk. Friendships are fastest broken when one of the parties owes the other money."

When he heard that, Angel had given her the quarter he received yesterday from the baker.

"I'll pay my own board," he said. "At least, as long as I can keep my job."

He expected that Raud would let him go. Certainly the Frenchman would have received a full account of Angel's conduct from his countrymen. But nothing was said about it when he reported for work on Monday.

Gradually his days settled into a rut. They started with a singing lesson, only now he was permitted to intersperse the hated scales with simple songs. When the professor, who had still not staked out his own claim, left to inspect the claims of others, Angel remained behind.

By that time, Mrs. Quin and Rowena had finished with their duties in the cabin and came outside to begin an endless laundry. The shirts and jeans, socks and underwear of various miners were scrubbed by hand with homemade soft soap, boiled over a fire, rinsed, and hung to dry on Red's clothesline and on every nearby bush. Angel helped. He carried water and brought wood for the fire, and all the time he sang, for singing was his part of the bargain, and he wanted to be like Red, someone who always kept his word.

He had learned to tell by the sun when it was time to leave for the bakery, and now the way did not seem nearly so long. His legs no longer ached at night, although news that Raud would now deliver bread had brought many new customers. Angel went first to the Leger Hotel, then to French Hill, and after that there were scattered cabins to visit.

Usually the old Chinese was sitting alone in front of his shack as he went by, but he had grown accustomed to seeing the boy with his baskets filled with brown loaves. The fear had gone from his eyes, and now when Angel said hello, the Chinese answered with a strange, incomprehensible word that must have been a greeting.

Sometimes Angel stopped a moment and they spoke, each in his own tongue, neither understanding the other's words, but exchanging friendly smiles. Once the old man had given him a present, three round, brown nuts that tasted sweet and not like nuts at all. They had exchanged names, too, each pointing to himself and speaking slowly.

The old man's name was Chung Far. Outside of that Angel knew nothing about him. He wondered how so old a man happened to be here, where all the men, particularly the Orientals, were young.

One Saturday when the last of the miners' washing was finished for the week, Rowena begged to go with him on his route. Some day, she pointed out, Angel might be sick and unable to make his deliveries. If she knew the routine, she could take over for him. Angel snorted derisively at the idea, but Mrs. Quin seemed to think it had merit.

"You watch over her, though, Angel," she cautioned. "A rough mining camp's no place for a young lady to be wandering about by herself."

"If I only had a gun, you wouldn't have to worry," said Rowena pointedly. "I could go any place I wanted."

Angel smiled to himself. Since he had learned that Red, too, was a little irritated by her boasting, it didn't bother him so much.

Monsieur Raud greeted Rowena politely, but he seemed upset. He gave her a raisin bun to eat, and called Angel into the kitchen where they could speak privately.

"It is not good to have the young lady with you today," he said gravely. "Perhaps she will stay here with me while you make your deliveries."

"What is it?" asked Angel in surprise. "What happened?"

"There has been a robbery and killing," explained Raud. "It happened sometime this morning. One of the Chinese was murdered. He was tied up by his own queue, and his throat was cut. The killer was doubtless trying to make him tell where the others had hidden their gold. We would not have known so soon, but one of the Chinese returned to his shack and found him there. He came running to Monsieur Leger with the news, who, in turn, told it to me."

"Chung Far," cried Angel in horror. "Was he old, the one who was killed?"

"I have told you all I know." Raud shrugged his shoulders. "But tonight, when the miners return and hear about it, a meeting will be held. Something must be done. It is a dreadful thing."

"Yes," agreed Angel weakly. He was sure it had been Chung Far. The old man always stayed alone when his countrymen went to their claims.

He remembered the first time he had seen Chung

155

Far, and the fear that had filled his eyes. He must have looked like that to the killer, a defenseless, terrified old man. Who could have been so cruel?

"So you see, it is better that the young lady is not about on such a day," concluded Raud. "She must stay with me."

Angel agreed, but Rowena did not. She was properly horrified at the account of the murder, but she argued that by now the killer was probably far away. There was no reason why she could not accompany Angel on his rounds as she had planned.

Raud finally had to give in.

"Young ladies are very different here," he observed in French. "At home they are modest and respect their elders. They do not thrust themselves pigheadedly into the face of danger. I wash my hands of you. Go. Go. Go."

Angel took up the baskets, already filled for the hotel. Since it was Saturday, the regular order was doubled. Many of the miners would begin their weekend by dining out tonight.

"We'll hurry," he promised Raud. "We won't stop for anything. We'll go just as fast as we can."

The baker nodded soberly.

It was a temptation not to linger in the hotel kitchen. The help had heard the story of the killing, and tongues were wagging busily.

"Was it an old man? The Chinese who is dead?" Angel asked one of the cooks, as he began unloading bread onto a table.

"Yes," answered the cook, launching immediately into a long explanation in rapid French, too intricate for

Angel to follow. He caught only two familiar words, Joaquin Murieta.

"It was Joaquin Murieta? The bandit?" he interrupted impatiently.

"Certainly."

"He was seen?" Remembrance of a thin, scarred face beneath a tall sombrero flashed through Angel's mind. Yes, that man would have no compunction about slaying a defenseless old Chinese.

"No," admitted the cook. Then he added triumphantly, "But who else could it be?"

Angel took the last loaf from the basket and turned to Rowena, who was staring wide-eyed at the huge stove with all its cooking pots and pans.

"Come on. We've got to hurry," he ordered brusquely.

When they returned to the bakery, Raud met them at the door.

"You will go only to my countrymen on French Hill. No single orders today. You must return that young lady to her home as soon as possible."

Angel nodded. He did not want a second meeting with the scar-faced Joaquin either, although considering the speed with which the bandit had taken off before, it was doubtful that he would still be around.

As they passed Chinatown, a young coolie was hanging strips of white cloth around the doorway of the last shack. He did not turn as they went by, but continued stolidly with his task.

"Wait," Angel told Rowena, and walked back to where the man was working.

"I just wanted to ask you a question," he began. The Chinese turned to regard him with blank eyes.

He was young, and dressed in the traditional blue jacket and long trousers of his people. His freshly washed barefeet were thrust into straw sandals, and the queue of hair that hung down his back was glossy black. The door behind him was ajar, and through the crack Angel could hear a murmur of muted voices and smell the odors of burning joss sticks.

"Was he—was it Chung Far who was killed?" Under the steady stare, Angel grew embarrassed and wished that he hadn't stopped.

"Chung Far." The man repeated the words, nodding.

"I'm sorry," said Angel. "He was my friend."

"Chung Far speak of you. Say you good boy. Always sing," the Chinese told him gravely, then turned to resume his work.

Angel continued on up the hill. His thoughts were so filled with bitterness that he hardly heard Rowena as she chattered away at his side. She seemed to be taking the whole thing very lightly, he told himself, but then, of course, she had never known Chung Far. To her it was just one of those terrible stories that you heard about, but which seemed very far away.

But it was real to Angel. He would never pass through Chinatown without remembering the old man.

To his relief, all the French miners were away this afternoon, so they did not lose time in conversation. Rowena wanted to explore the camp, but he hurried her off as soon as he put the bread on the table. Now he was beginning to agree with the baker. A girl belonged at home with her mother when there was evil about.

He raced her back down the hill so fast that she complained. Another time he would have had more sympathy, but not now. Mrs. Quin had made it quite clear that Rowena was Angel's responsibility. He had to get her home safely.

Raud handed over the day's wages, with compliments on the speed of their trip.

"Now I can breathe again. Get her home quickly," he advised.

"Yes, sir, I will," promised Angel, pushing Rowena before him out of the door.

But once outside, she refused to be hurried any more.

"This is silly," she declared indignantly. "Everything that's going to happen already has. The town's deserted. Or almost. There's only one person on the street, down there by the livery barn. And he looks harmless enough."

Angel's eyes followed her pointing finger. A moment later, his scowl had changed to a delighted smile of recognition. Even from this distance there was no mistaking the man who was advancing toward them. It was the friend he had sought so long, his benefactor on the night of the Hounds. It was Joaquin!

"I know him," he cried joyfully. "He's my friend. We'll be safe with him." Then he started running down the rough walkway, shouting Joaquin's name.

The approaching Mexican frowned a little in his attempts to recall this stranger who seemed to know him. He was over medium height and very slender, but the jacket of dark red velvet clung to powerfully muscled shoulders. Beneath it was an embroidered shirt of white silk, and his high-heeled boots glistened in the sunlight. He wore his black hair shoulder length, and on his head was a white sombrero, elaborated with silver to match the silver trimmings on a gun belt which swung low

159

about his slender hips. He stopped in the road as Angel reached him, and smiled down questioningly at the excited boy.

"You know me?"

"Yes, yes," cried Angel in disappointment. How could Joaquin fail to recognize him? "I'm Angel. Angel Palma. Don't you remember that night in San Francisco on Telegraph Hill? On Loma Linda? You and Rosita took me into your tent. I stayed there with you all night. The Hounds below were killing my people. The Chileans."

"I do remember." The black eyes in the handsome face lightened, and Joaquin smiled warmly. "I remember the small boy who stayed with us that night. I've wondered since what happened to you."

"I'm so glad to see you," Angel told him simply. "Afterward, I wished I'd come with you when you asked me to."

"You did not find your mother," guessed Joaquin. When Angel shook his head, he added sympathetically, "I was afraid it would be so. But now you look happy and well fed. You are clothed. You have friends, someone to care for you."

"Yes," admitted Angel. Only a few weeks ago he would not have made that reply. He would have told Joaquin that he was alone, that he wanted to join him. But that was when he thought Joaquin was the famous bandit, and that bandits were people to be admired. That was before he had met Red Kirk.

"Humph." Rowena had come up beside him, and now she kicked at his ankle, demanding recognition.

"This is Rowena Quin," said Angel, a little grudgingly. "I've been staying with her folks and Red. Red Kirk," he added proudly. "Rowena, this is my friend Joaquin—Joaquin—"

"Sanchez," supplied the Mexican quickly. The magnificent white sombrero was lifted from his head as he made a deep bow. "Señorita, it is my great pleasure."

"Are you pretty good with those guns?" Rowena bobbed a polite curtsy, but her eyes had never left the two silver pistols in his gun belt.

For a moment Joaquin stared in amazement. Then he laughed and slid one of the guns from its holster.

"I am fair, señorita," he admitted modestly. "But these are for show. For decoration. A gambler requires many trappings. He must stand out handsomely in the crowd. That is why I wear these. They are small, as you see, and not much use."

Angel felt his face burn with embarrassment. He had never been so angry with Rowena as he was right now. Joaquin was *his* friend. They had much to say to one another. How dared she interrupt with her talk about guns.

"Could I look at it, please?" Rowena held out her hand, and after a second Joaquin handed her the pistol.

"Be careful, señorita. It is loaded."

"Oh, she's an expert," growled Angel scornfully. "She can hit a grizzly bear in his left eye."

"So?" Joaquin's thin eyebrows raised in surprise.

"Maybe not with this," admitted Rowena. She was examining the pistol carefully. "Not the first time, anyway. You see, I've never shot with anything but a rifle."

"So you became a gambler?" asked Angel, desperately trying to get the conversation away from Rowena and guns. "Where do you gamble, Joaquin?"

161

"On Saturday nights and Sundays I deal monte at the Leger Hotel." He answered absently, for his eyes were on Rowena. "Would you like to try the pistol, señorita? If we go back down the street, away from the building, we could find a safe target."

"Oh, yes," she accepted eagerly.

"We can't," objected Angel. "I've got to get her home. Probably you haven't heard, but there was a murder here this morning. The killer may still be around."

"A murder?" Joaquin looked at him closely.

"It was a nice old Chinese who never hurt anybody." Angel's voice was bitter. "They think whoever did it was trying to make him tell where the other Chinese had hidden their gold dust."

"It is likely," Joaquin nodded. "The Chinese are good miners. They are often attacked this way. But by now, whoever did it would be far away from here. Surely you have time to let the señorita try the pistol. It seems to mean a great deal to her."

"Angel's a scaredy cat," declared Rowena disdainfully.

"I am not," he denied. "Go ahead and shoot it, if you have to. I've been wanting to see you miss, anyway. After this, maybe you won't brag so much."

But Rowena did not miss. Her first shot hit the tree trunk which they had decided upon as a target.

"Too low." She frowned. "That wasn't where I meant it to go."

"It was very good." Joaquin applauded in surprise, while Angel could only stare.

"I was aiming for that knot higher up," she explained. "I'll try again."

This time she hit the mark exactly, and the next time, and the next.

"You are a natural shot, señorita," cried Joaquin in admiration. "Who taught you?"

"A mountain man named Zeb Grant." Rowena's cheeks were pink with excitement, and her eyes sparkled. "I used his rifle, and my shoulder was always black and blue afterwards. This is lots better. I've never used a pistol before. I wish I had one."

"You have," said Joaquin promptly. "It would be a shame for anyone who shoots as well as you to be without. That is yours."

"Oh, but I couldn't take it," Rowena told him sadly. "It isn't right to accept presents from a stranger."

"But I am not a stranger," he assured her gallantly. "At least, not to Angel. We are old friends. And since Angel is a friend of yours, I make this present to you through our mutual friend."

"Well—" Rowena hesitated only a moment before she smiled her happy acceptance of the gift.

"Come on," said Angel gruffly. "I better get you home before your mother's worried. I'll come and see you, Joaquin," he called over his shoulder. "We have lots to talk about, when there's no show-off around to hog the conversation."

Chapter 13

Much to Angel's amazement, little was done about Chung Far's murder. When the miners heard about it, they shook their heads and agreed that it was a dastardly crime but that it was much too late to apprehend the criminal. Besides, it wasn't as though it had happened to one of them. It was just some old Chinaman no one knew. Universally, however, they all took extra precautions about hiding their own gold dust, for if Joaquin Murieta was in these parts—and everyone agreed it had to be Murieta—a man couldn't be too careful.

Even Mrs. Quin, who was properly horrified at the wanton slaying, was more concerned about the propriety of Rowena accepting a silver-handled pistol as a gift.

"It's not a nice thing to give a young lady," she declared, pursing her mouth with disapproval. "And it's not proper for a young lady to accept anything so valuable, especially from a stranger."

"But he wasn't a stranger, Mama," argued Rowena. "At least not to Angel. If it hadn't been for Angel, the man wouldn't have given it to me."

"I didn't know you were well acquainted with anybody around these parts, Angel." She looked at him sharply.

"Joaquin's my friend," he told her. "I've known him a long time. And there wasn't anything he could do but give it to her, not after she took on the way she did."

"Joaquin," repeated Red thoughtfully. "He's the one who helped you out in Frisco. So you finally caught up with him. What's he doing for a living? Did he say?"

"He deals monte at the hotel," explained Angel quickly. For a moment he was afraid that Red might say too much, but as he looked into the quizzical blue eyes he knew his friend would never do that. "His name's Joaquin Sanchez. He said for me to come and see him and we could talk some more. Alone," he added significantly, glaring at Rowena.

She was fondling the silver handle of the pistol, tracing the engraving with one finger, and did not appear to hear him.

"A gambler," gasped Mrs. Quin. "That makes it even worse. Thaddeus, are you going to let our daughter accept presents from a gambler?"

"A man's worth is not always measured by his present occupation," he reminded her in throbbing tones. "A small gift—a token gesture—to a little girl—"

"Let me see that gun." Red reached out one huge hand, and Rowena reluctantly gave it to him.

"This would come in mighty handy for small game," decided the miner after a moment. "Rabbits and squirrels and such as go into stews. It wouldn't count much with anything so big as a bear. I don't know as it would even kill a man, but it would at least make him mighty unhappy. Fair balance to it, too."

"I could get us all kinds of game, Mama," tempted Rowena eagerly. "Think how good it would taste. Of course," she added cannily, "I'd have to have some bullets. Mr. Sanchez didn't give me any of them."

"I should think not," declared Mrs. Quin. After a moment she gave in. "Well, if you really think it's all right, Thaddeus. And if Mr. Kirk doesn't believe it would cause talk for Rowena to accept such a present—"

"And you'll buy the bullets, won't you?" cried Rowena, running to throw her arms around her mother's neck. "Oh, Mama! Oh, I'm so happy. Oh, I wish Zeb Grant was here!"

Angel turned away and went to stand in the door. Well, it would be nice to have meat stews, he told himself. And, as Rowena had pointed out, Joaquin had merely given a gift to someone he thought was a mutual friend. She should really thank Angel for the gun.

He did not ask the Quins' permission to visit the gaming room of the hotel the next weekend, but he did consult Red Kirk. In San Francisco, the orphans were barred from these places of entertainment, and big-muscled men stood by to make sure that none slipped through the door. After the occasion when he had tried to make off with the miner's gun, Angel did not care to break any local rules.

"Never heard of any such law around here," said Red gravely. "Mainly because you're about the only young 'un about, saving a few babes in arms. But I don't reckon your friend'll have any time for visiting. He's a dealer."

"I told him I would come," said Angel, ignoring the last remark.

"You say anything to Mrs. Quin about it? Or the professor?" asked Red.

"No, sir." Angel met the blue eyes honestly. "Mrs. Quin would have a fit. There's no sense in worrying her. And the professor's been so busy lately with his new friend that he can hardly wait to finish with my singing lesson before he rushes off to see him."

"Snuffy Ballard," nodded Red thoughtfully. "Last person in the world I expected the professor to take to. And I never knowed Snuffy to cotton up to anybody before this, neither. He's that cantankerous he'll scarce give the time of day to the banker when he turns in his dust on Sunday. But they say him and the professor jaw away like a couple of magpies all day long, Snuffy rocking away at his cradle and the professor sitting there on the bank, watching."

"Joaquin's only there Saturday nights and Sunday," interrupted Angel, bringing the subject back to his visit to the hotel. "I thought I'd go tonight."

"Maybe it'd be best if I went along," decided Red after a moment. "Not that there's likely to be complaints, but if there is, I could vouch for you."

"Thanks," said Angel gratefully. He had never known a more understanding friend than Red. In some ways he was even better than Pierre.

Angel was disappointed with his first inspection of the gambling room of the Leger Hotel. He had expected it to more nearly approximate the glittering glimpses revealed when the doors swung wide on similar establishments of Portsmouth Square. Here were no crystal chandeliers, only oil lamps; no thickly carpeted or polished-tile floors, only rough boards; no vivid paintings on the bare walls. But there was a long mirror running the entire length of the crowded bar, and there were Mexican fandango girls wearing brightly colored skirts, which twirled gaily when they danced in the microscopic space between the gaming tables.

The room was crowded with tables of various sizes. Some were surrounded by chairs, but the patrons stood around others, elbowing each other for room as they watched the play of cards. One thing it did have in common with the more luxurious gaming houses of San Francisco was its noise. Men shouted and laughed as loudly here, and in the occasional tense stillnesses, while players held their breaths awaiting the turn of dice or cards, Angel could even hear a snatch of music. Someone was playing a harmonica.

Red looked down at him and grinned.

"How's it strike you?"

"It's pretty crowded," admitted Angel uncertainly. He had been afraid that someone would stop him at the door, but he hadn't expected the other extreme. No one had even noticed he was there. He wondered how he could find Joaquin in all this maze of pushing, shouting miners.

"The monte tables is over here," said Red, as though reading his thoughts. "That long one yonder against the wall's for lansquenet. Likely you'll find your friend Raud playing there, if you want to say howdy. It's all the Frenchies play. In between's tables for faro and euchre and so on."

"The monte table," decided Angel quickly.

Red's big body made a wedge to clear a path through the crowd and Angel followed close behind. Some of the miners objected vigorously to giving way, but when they turned and recognized the tall miner, their anger turned to good nature. Red Kirk was well liked on Mok Hill.

There were several tables devoted to the Mexican game of monte, and Red looked down inquiringly as they neared each one. At the first two Angel shook his head, but at the third he began to smile. The dealer was Joaquin.

At first Joaquin did not see them. His black head was tilted to one side, his eyes on the cards that he dealt. The nimble brown fingers moved so swiftly that Angel found himself blinking in his efforts to follow. He had no understanding of the game, and he could only stare in bewilderment as the miners sorted their hands and discarded some of the cards. Finally Joaquin turned up a single card from the deck.

"Diamonds, señores," he announced gently.

Two of the miners tossed away their hands and stood up.

"Monte ain't my game tonight," declared one of them. "Think I'll try faro."

"Better luck, señores," Joaquin called after them as he began scooping up coins from the table.

It seemed to be the end of the game and an appropriate time to make himself known, so Angel slid through the opening left by the departing players.

"Hello, Joaquin," he said shyly.

This time the gambler had no trouble recognizing

him. In his thin brown face, white teeth flashed a welcoming smile.

"My little friend," he said cordially. "My little friend of the tragic night. I did not expect to see you here."

"But I said I'd come," explained Angel in surprise. "We were going to talk."

"But now I am working," explained Joaquin. His brown eyes grew sad. "I should have made myself clearer. When I deal monte I cannot visit, not even with so old a friend as you."

"I tried to tell you, boy." Red's huge hand descended on Angel's shoulder comfortingly. "The man's got a job to do."

"I am sorry," said Joaquin.

"Maybe I could come to see you at your house," suggested Angel unhappily. "You and Rosita."

"Rosita is at Contreras—Mex Town," amended Joaquin quickly. "She will be glad to see you. I am there sometimes, but often I am away during the week. I have many relatives scattered around the country upon whom I must pay my respects. A duty, you understand."

"Are we going to play monte or not?" grumbled one of the miners, and with an apologetic smile at Angel, Joaquin's fingers began shuffling cards.

Red sat down in one of the recently vacated chairs.

"Think I'll take a hand," he decided. "Feel kind of lucky tonight. Don't wander off too far, boy."

For a few minutes Angel watched the game, but he couldn't figure out the rules. Joaquin and Red were so absorbed that they seemed to have forgotten all about him. When, by some miracle, a passageway opened in the crowd, he decided to venture out on his own. His objective was the opposite end of the room where, from time to time, had come those snatches of music.

At the far end of the bar was an empty space beside the door leading to the hotel dining room. It was too small to accommodate a gaming table, but there was ample room for one chair. This was occupied by a small man who wore voluminous pantaloons and a frayed shirt which had once been red but was now faded to a dusky pink. On his head was a derby hat without a crown, and through the opening rose a glistening, hairless dome. At the moment he was playing a harmonica, but on the floor beside him was a violin.

Angel advanced to a position directly in front of the musician and stood listening carefully. The man was playing one of Mrs. Quin's favorite songs, 'Home Sweet Home.' It must have been one of the men's favorites, too, for those nearby put down their cards to listen and their eyes grew sad. When he finished, the player removed the harmonica from his mouth and thrust it into his pocket.

"That's not easy," he announced proudly. "Lots of folks think they're pretty good on a jew's-harp, but let 'em try that with all the froufraws."

"It was beautiful," said Angel.

"You want to make a request?" asked the man. "Some special number you like? Brandy Wiener—that's me—can play any tune he's ever heard. If I ain't heard it, then you sing it through once and I can play it. What'll it be?"

"Oh, anything you want to play," said Angel quickly. "I like everything but scales."

"Scales!" Brandy spat contemptuously on the floor. "Scales is for beginners that has to learn by note. Me, I was born with music in me. It just comes out."

Angel wished that Professor Quin agreed with that theory.

"Reckon it's about time to give them 'Hangtown Gals' again," decided Brandy, reaching for the violin on the floor. "Have to do that ever so often during a night, but it goes better on the fiddle. The customers get to singing along, and it puts them in a good humor so they forget their losses."

"Could I sing, too?" Angel's eyes sparkled. It would be fun to sing again to a musical accompaniment. Of course, one musician couldn't compare with the whole of Jake Plumber's band, but it was better than nothing.

"It's a free country," shrugged Brandy, drawing the bow across the strings to test their accuracy.

He began the rollicking melody beloved by the miners, and Angel joined in.

> "Hangtown gals are plump and rosy
> Hair in ringlets, mighty cozy,
> Painted cheeks and jossy bonnets
> Touch 'em and they'll sting like hornets.
> Hangtown gals are lovely creatures
> Think they'll marry Mormon preachers
> Heads thrown back to show their features
>   Ha, ha, ha, Hangtown gals!"

From all sides of the room voices took up the lyrics, and, by the time they had reached the end of the many

verses, it had become a loud, echoing roar, but everyone was smiling. As Brandy said, it put them in a good humor.

The musician, however, frowned throughout. At first he leaned closer to Angel, as though he might be trying to listen, but as the voices rose he straightened up and continued on to the end. Now, as the customers returned happily to their games, he turned to the boy.

"You got a fair voice. Know anything else?"

"Oh, yes," said Angel eagerly, and rattled off the titles of some of Mrs. Quin's songs.

"Let's try 'Briny O'Lynn,'" decided Brandy, and immediately began the introduction.

After that they did 'Robin Adair' and 'Cherry Ripe' and 'Believe Me if All Those Endearing Young Charms' while Brandy shifted from violin to harmonica, whichever he deemed the proper accompaniment for the selection. They had been so intent on each other and their own performances that neither had noticed that the roar of voices about them had died away. It was a shock when their last song was greeted by the thundering applause of clapping hands and stamping feet. This was followed by a handful of coins, quarters, half dollars, Mexican pesos, even a small nugget or two which fell around them.

Angel could only stare in astonishment, but Brandy was equal to the occasion.

"Requests, gents," he called, gathering up money as fast as possible. "You name it. We do it. Always aim to please."

Requests came fast and furious. The Frenchmen at the lansquenet table wanted 'The Marseillaise.' Luckily, it was one of the few songs Angel had learned from Pierre, and when he sang it in French, the Ingots all stood at attention. The Mexicans called out their favorites, and the Germans and the Americans. Brandy was never at a loss, but Angel had never heard of many of them

174

and had to stand silently while the harmonica or violin complied. Whenever this happened, the listeners grew restive. Brandy knew it and made his solos as brief as possible. It was the vocal numbers that resulted in the largest showers of tossed coins.

At last, Monsieur Leger, the proprietor, hurried over.

"This is enough entertainment for now, Brandy," he whispered. "The games make the money for the house. But it was a treat. A drawing card."

"You better believe it," growled Brandy. "They'll come back for more."

"I shall not forget," promised Monsieur Leger hastily. He turned to Angel. "How would you like to sing weekly? On Saturday nights and Sunday at the glorious Leger Hotel?"

"For money?" gasped Angel.

"Certainly for money," said Brandy. "And my salary'll have to go up, too. There's a lot of requests the boy don't know, and if I have to learn him, it'll cost something."

Monsieur Leger threw up his hands helplessly at the demand, and at that moment Red Kirk elbowed his way through the crowd and reached their side.

"That was fine, Angel," he cried enthusiastically. "I'd no idea you could sing so good. Everybody thought it was fine. Your friend Joaquin he broke down and cried when you did that Mexican thing."

"Mr. Leger just offered me a job, Red," cried Angel happily. "He wants me to sing here every Saturday night and Sunday. And Mr. Brandy will teach me the songs I don't know."

Red's face lost its wide smile.

"Maybe you can't say yes to that, Angel," he said soberly. "You got a commitment to Professor Quin. His bargain with you was about your singing. You'll have to ask him first."

Chapter 14

"I really see nothing wrong with it. In some ways, the proposal has great merit," decided Professor Quin thoughtfully. "Of course, as the boy's manager and mentor, I myself would have to investigate the matter more fully and make all arrangements with the proprietor of the establishment."

Angel had been holding his breath. Now it came out in a great gasp of relief.

"Well, if you don't see something wrong with it, Thaddeus Quin, I do." Mrs. Quin's brown eyes snapped angrily. "The idea of letting a young boy sing in a saloon! And while we're on the subject, Mr. Kirk, I'm surprised at you, taking him there last night the way you did."

"My dear, my dear." The professor used his most soothing tones. "I agree that it is not what we would like, but we must be content with small beginnings. Remember that the mightiest oak sprang from a small acorn."

There was nothing to worry about, Angel told himself. The professor approved of the singing job at the hotel, and eventually he would persuade his wife. He always had. It was only recently that Mrs. Quin was proving a little stubborn on certain points.

"I do declare, Thaddeus, lately it seems that you've taken leave of your senses," she exclaimed, and Angel could tell that she was switching to one of those points now. "Things that would rile a normal man don't bother you one whit! Like staying on here, and crowding poor Mr. Kirk, when you've had plenty of time to build us a cabin of our own. And not filing on a claim when that was the whole purpose of us coming to this place!"

"You're not crowding me none, Mrs. Quin," the miner assured her quickly. He had grown red when she scolded him about taking Angel to the hotel, and he seemed relieved that she had changed the subject. "It's a pleasure having you."

"But what'll it be when it turns cold? Will it still be such a pleasure sleeping in an open shed? And that's not all, Thaddeus," she continued indignantly. "I've never before known you to take up with somebody like that Mr. Ballard, even bringing him home to supper like you did!"

"This is not like you, Almira," chided the professor. "Is it Christian charity to deny food to a hungry man?"

"It isn't the food, Papa. It's the way he smells," put in Rowena slyly, but they did not seem to hear.

"Mr. Ballard can afford to buy his own meals," re-

178

torted Mrs. Quin snappishly. "People say he's the richest man on Mok Hill. Isn't that right, Mr. Kirk?"

"Snuffy never says what he's worth, ma'am." Red refused to be drawn into the argument. He began sidling toward the door, and a significant raise of his bushy eyebrows suggested that Angel join him outside.

Angel was glad to comply. The Quins might be at it for some time. It seemed that every day they went round and round on these same subjects, of the professor filing on his own claim, building his own cabin, and his new friendship with the taciturn Snuffy Ballard. Like Red, Angel kept silent during the arguments, but he secretly sided with Mrs. Quin. The professor should have staked out a claim by this time and provided living quarters for his own family. And why he wanted to sit on the bank day after day, watching Snuffy Ballard rock his cradle, Angel couldn't imagine. Maybe it was because Snuffy didn't talk much. People said Professor Quin spent a lot of time reciting poetry, and maybe Snuffy was a good listener.

"Whew," said Red, wiping the back of his neck with a freshly laundered bandanna. "I get hot under the collar every time them two start in. As nice a little woman as Mrs. Quin is, wouldn't you think he'd be willing to give just a little, once in a while?"

"I hope he doesn't give in about letting me sing at the hotel," worried Angel.

"Not likely," decided Red. Then he added thoughtfully, "He's got something up his sleeve, though, and I'd give a cookie to know what it is."

Angel attended church services with the Quins that

morning, then he and the professor left together for the Leger Hotel.

The room had changed little since last night. It was still noisy and crowded and smelled of perspiring bodies and the cheap perfume of the fandango girls. Angel wondered if the customers had just stayed on through the night and not even bothered to go home.

"Where will we find the proprietor?" Professor Quin had to bend down and shout in Angel's ear to make himself heard.

"I don't know," shouted Angel in return. "But Brandy Wiener's at the other end of the room. I think I heard his fiddle."

The professor nodded, and with a great swoop of his arm indicated that the boy was to lead the way.

It seemed less crowded at the side devoted to lansquenet, so Angel started ahead to the right. The long table, occupied by the Ingots last night, was vacant, but they evidently were expected back, for every chair was tilted forward against the table top. He hoped they would return before he sang. The Frenchmen had been most liberal with their coins when he finished 'The Marseillaise.'

Brandy saw them coming. He concluded 'Old Dan Tucker' with a flourish, and put the violin carefully on the floor beside him.

"You're early, boy." His dry voice was critical. "Monsoor won't want you till later on. We got to give the customers a chance to lose a little first."

"You may introduce us, Angel," permitted the professor grandly.

"This is Professor Quin. He says it's all right for me

to sing. This is Mr. Wiener. He can play any tune he's ever heard on the fiddle and jew's-harp both," added Angel enviously. "You ought to hear him do 'Annie Laurie.'"

"I should like to," admitted the professor. "Perhaps, sir, you will give me a sample of your artistry."

Brandy looked at him sharply before taking the harmonica from his pocket. Then he played 'Annie Laurie,' followed by other numbers. Some were suggested by the professor, and although Angel had never heard of them, Brandy instantly complied.

"You are somewhat versatile," decided Professor Quin.

"I'm the best in the country." Brandy glared at him angrily. "You know anybody else in California that comes anywheres near me?"

"No," said the professor quickly. His voice grew warm and deeply respectful. "Indeed, you are a great artist, Mr. Wiener. Talented to the nth degree."

Before long the professor wandered off to find Monsieur Leger, but Angel stayed behind. Even though it was difficult to hear above the noise, he enjoyed listening to the music. Only once did Brandy pay any attention to him.

"Actor, ain't he?" he asked, jerking his head in the direction taken by the departed Professor Quin.

"He's a professor of elocution and singing."

"He's one of them actors," insisted Brandy stubbornly. "I met up with them before."

Later in the afternoon, Angel was permitted to sing. His reception was the same as the night before. The gaming ceased, and requests were shouted loudly from every side of the room. Monsieur Leger and Professor

181

Quin, who apparently had reached an amiable agreement, stood by and watched. The proprietor kept nodding his head and smiling, but the professor's face was grave and thoughtful.

Angel was only allowed to sing for ten minutes, for Monsieur Leger wished the games to continue.

"But you will sing again this evening," he promised. "Once in the afternoon and twice in the evening we will give our customers a little treat. We will announce it beforehand. It will be something to which they will look forward when they come to the magnificent Leger Hotel."

Angel felt very proud. Now he had two jobs, delivering bread for Monsieur Raud and singing weekends at the hotel. He wondered how much Monsieur Leger meant to pay him. The professor had made the arrangements and he himself had not been consulted.

"Is it permissible for Mr. Wiener to take a brief rest?" The professor was using his richest, most persuasive tones. "An artist performs better after an occasional rest period, and I should like to consult with him concerning songs. Perhaps I may be of some help in teaching the boy certain lyrics that he does not know."

Monsieur Leger smiled and agreed that Brandy might stop playing for a few minutes while in consultation about songs. As he trotted away, the professor turned to Angel.

"You run along too. Go outside and fill your lungs with fresh air. Since you will not sing again until evening, perhaps it would be well to go home and return later. There is nothing to keep you here."

It was a clear dismissal, but one that Angel could not understand. If the two men were going to talk about songs, he ought to be here. After all, he was the one who would be singing.

"Run along," repeated Professor Quin, frowning. "What I have to say to Mr. Wiener is private."

Angel turned away angrily. He pushed through the crowd, using his elbows to force a passage. For the moment he forgot that Professor Quin was his benefactor, and he almost hated him. He wished that Red was here, but Red had stayed home today. Mrs. Quin had taken his gold dust to the bank, for Red had started building a fourth wall to the shed where the men slept. He claimed it was something he had always meant to do, but Angel knew it was because the professor showed no intention of building his own cabin. Well, he'd go home and help Red. It's what he'd really wanted to do anyway.

On his way out, he passed the monte tables. Today a strange Mexican occupied the dealer's chair where Joaquin had sat last night. That was strange, Angel told himself. His friend had said that he worked there every weekend. Perhaps something was wrong.

He squeezed through tiny openings, jabbing with elbows until a solid back gave way and let him through. When he reached the table he stood behind the dealer, waiting patiently till the game was at an end. As the Mexican began sweeping in coins and dust from the table, Angel touched him on the shoulder.

"Where is Joaquin?" he asked the startled brown face, which turned quickly. Without thinking, he spoke in Spanish. "This is his table. He's the regular dealer. Is he sick?"

"Yes, he is sick," agreed the substitute instantly. At

first he seemed a little nervous, but the sight of the boy seemed to reassure him and he smiled. "You are the one who sang," he recognized.

"Yes," agreed Angel. "Joaquin is my friend. I hope it is not serious, this sickness."

"No." The brown eyes almost twinkled. "A small sickness only. Enough to keep him this afternoon. He will be here tonight. I sit in for him only until then."

"That's good." Angel smiled in relief. "I'll see him then."

"You will see him then. Everyone will see him," promised the Mexican, and returned to the next deal.

By the time Angel had made his way outside he had reached a decision. Instead of returning to Red's cabin, he would spend the afternoon in Mex Town. Joaquin would be there and they could visit, returning together to the hotel that evening. Since Joaquin had to make so many duty calls on relatives during the week, it might be their only opportunity.

He set out at once, and the bitterness caused by Professor Quin's dismissal was almost erased from his mind.

The little cluster of houses occupied by the Mexicans was quite a distance. Angel had never been there, but he knew the way. He thought of Chung Far, as he always did when he passed through Chinatown. Today the Chinese were not mining, but were all behind tightly closed doors. He could hear their high-pitched voices, muffled by thick planks, and he wondered what they did on their days off. No one knew about the Orientals. They kept to themselves.

As he passed the familiar turnoff to French Hill, he

thought about the Ingots. Everyone knew what they did on Sunday. They played lansquenet at the hotel. They were playing it there now, for shortly after his own arrival they had marched in, resplendent in their blue and white Sunday uniforms, to claim the chairs that had been tilted against the table top.

Angel liked the Frenchmen. They had been kind to him. Raud had given him a job, and the others had kept the miners from whipping him the day he stole the rifle. He particularly liked Louis Renald, who seemed to be the youngest of the group. Now that he thought of it, Louis had not been among the players at the lansquenet table today. Angel wondered if he had been taken by another chill.

Then he climbed up and down another slope, and before him lay Mex Town. Angel would have known it anywhere.

The Mexicans had begun their settlement by building adobe houses, but the winter rains had necessitated certain alterations. The original adobe was now patched with sticks, pieces of stone, and jagged lengths of tin from old cans. Chickens scratched in the pounded dirt of the street, and children played in front of the buildings, watched over by their mothers who gossiped in the shade. A mongrel dog scented his approach and began yapping an alarm, which was instantly taken up by a dozen others. Angel smiled to himself and continued on. The Mexicans, he felt, were closest to the Chileans. It was a little like coming home.

The children left off playing, and the women stopped talking as he drew near. He could feel their eyes on him, staring suspiciously and he began to feel a little uncomfortable. These were not like the people he had known on Telegraph Hill. To these Mexicans, he was a stranger, a gringo, an outsider. But he continued on up to the group of women, and raising his voice above the noise of the dogs he addressed them in Spanish.

"Good afternoon, ladies. I come seeking my friend Joaquin."

"Joaquin who?" demanded one of the women suspiciously. "We have more than one Joaquin here."

"Joaquin Sanchez," he told her with dignity. "I am Angel Palma, and—"

"Angel! The boy from San Francisco. The boy who shared our tent!" One of the women jumped to her feet and rushed over to throw her arms around him. "Joaquin told me he had seen you. He said you were well, and grown so he hardly knew you. Nor did I."

"Rosita!"

He hadn't recognized her, either, and he could hardly do so now as she held him out at arm's length, smiling into his face. True, she was still slender and pretty, but the woman he remembered had been frail and as frightened as he. This one stood with an air of assurance and pride. The Rosita he remembered had worn a cheap cotton dress and a faded rebozo. This one was dressed in silk, with lace about her shoulders, a gold chain about her neck, and bracelets on her arms.

"Is it really you?" he wondered aloud.

"It is I." Rosita laughed merrily. Then she turned to the others. "Angel is an old friend. You will excuse us while we go to my house and talk."

The other women nodded respectfully, and Angel

observed that none was as richly dressed as Rosita or
rivaled her in poise and assurance. Even the dogs seemed
to sense her authority, for they had left off barking as she
spoke.

The hut where she led him looked much like the
others before they entered, but inside it stopped being
a hut. There was a thick carpet on the floor, and one
wall held a shrine while another was almost concealed
by an oil painting in a gold frame. In one corner was a
wide bed with a silken coverlet, and in the center
stood a dark, carved oak table with matching chairs
cushioned in velvet. Angel had never been in so fine a

room before, and when Rosita motioned him to a seat, he could only sit and stare.

"You like my house?" Rosita laughed gently. "It is yours."

Angel understood that this was only a Spanish phrase of politeness, and he nodded respectfully. To earn the money to pay for all this, Joaquin must be a very talented monte dealer.

"I have other beautiful houses in other towns." Rosita could not refrain from boasting a little as she watched his wide eyes turning this way and that. Then she added kindly, "But sometimes I have no house at all. Sometimes we travel long distances, and I have not even a tent. I sleep beneath the trees."

"I'd never leave here," he assured her solemnly. "Never."

"I could not let Joaquin go alone. He travels much. Where he goes, I go with him."

"Where is he?" Angel's eyes turned to the empty bed. "He was not at his table today, so I came to see him here. I've been wanting to talk to him, and you, too, of course," he added.

"He is not here today," Rosita told him. "He went to West Point. An old aunt was taken ill. She sent for her favorite nephew, my Joaquin. But it is less than a day's ride. He will return early this evening."

"The dealer at his table said Joaquin was sick," remembered Angel. "That's why I came. He said he wasn't very sick, only a little."

"That Pepe!" Rosita laughed gaily. "He did not know you, or he would have told the truth. It is better to say that you yourself are sick than that you go to make a call upon someone else. Perhaps Pepe thought you were from the management. That you were sent to make inquiries."

"That's probably it," agreed Angel. It seemed a logical explanation.

"But you will see Joaquin," promised Rosita. "You will stay and have supper with us. He will be back late this afternoon, in—let me see—" She pulled on the gold chain around her neck, and a watch slipped from her waist. "In about two hours," she finished, closing the watch and sliding it back into place. "Visit with me for two hours. Then Joaquin will come, and there will still be another hour before he relieves Pepe at the hotel."

Angel stood up. He shook his head, forcing onto his face the look of blankness that he had learned from the orphans so long ago.

"I am sorry. I cannot stay." It was hard to keep emotion from his voice. It sounded strange and forced to him, but luckily Rosita did not notice. "I only stopped to say hello. I must go now."

"You will come back?" She followed him to the door, calling after him. "Come see us again. My house is always your house."

Angel nodded, but he could not trust himself to speak. He hurried outside, past the staring women, the open-mouthed children, the silent dogs, down the street which soon became a trail.

Not until he was out of sight of the settlement did he slow down. Then he stopped, leaning his head against the trunk of a tree, and allowed himself to think.

How had Rosita come by that gold watch? Had she bought it, or found it, or received it as a present? He had wanted to ask, but somehow he couldn't. Of course, he might have been mistaken, but he didn't think so. He was almost sure it was Professor Quin's gold watch, the one that had been taken from him by the bandit Joaquin the day the stagecoach was held up.

Chapter 15

Angel stood by the tree for a long time. After the heat of the sun the shade felt cool. He could hear little rustlings in the woods behind him, and he wondered absently if it could be a bear. It didn't seem important.

The important question was how Rosita had acquired Professor Quin's gold watch. There were several explanations, and Angel's mind explored them all. Maybe the killer had dropped it, and she had found it. Maybe Joaquin had won it in a monte game. Maybe he had bought it for her. One by one, Angel had to discard each one. There had to be some connection between his friend and the bandit who had killed the stagecoach driver.

He remembered that Red had claimed that there was more than one bandit operating under the name of Joaquin, since robberies were committed simultaneously twenty or thirty miles apart. Red must be right. There were two of them, working singly. But which was the good one? Which was the leader Murieta, the hero of the Mexicans on Telegraph Hill? It had to be Angel's Joaquin, of course, otherwise the watch would not have been turned over to him.

For just a moment, Angel felt a return of that old feeling of pride for his friend. No matter what people said, there were excusable reasons to make a man steal. Mexicans had it hard in California. The old ranchos, which had been their livelihood, were gone. They couldn't take out claims, the way Red and the other miners did, because they were foreigners and wouldn't pay the tax. Only a few of the lucky ones, like Joaquin, had jobs dealing monte. . . . He turned away from this line of thought. It was disloyal to remember that Joaquin had money to pay the tax and that he was a bandit by choice. Anyway, he was a good bandit. He wouldn't kill anyone.

The other one now, the bad Joaquin, was a different matter. Somehow, someway, Angel had to find a means of separating him from the good Joaquin and bringing him to justice. The watch was a clue. The two must meet occasionally, perhaps right here on Mok Hill. But how to capture one without incriminating the other?

He ought to tell the professor about the watch, but that was out of the question. He wished he could take Red into his confidence, but that, too, was impossible. If only Pierre were here, he would understand. But Pierre was far away, locked up in Sam Brannan's orphan asylum.

It was a difficult problem, and one that he would have to solve alone. Moreover, he'd have to do something about it soon. He couldn't allow the bad Joaquin to continue, freely killing innocent people like the stage-coach driver and Chung Far.

As he neared the turnoff to French Hill, he realized that he would arrive back in town with nothing to do. There was no longer time to go to the cabin before he was due at the hotel. Also, there was the matter of his stomach. He had been too occupied with the problem to notice before, but he was very hungry. If only it weren't Sunday, he could stop at the bakery and Raud would give him a bun, but on Sunday Raud played lansquenet at the hotel. All the Frenchmen had been there today, except Louis Renald. His chair had stood empty.

Angel nodded to himself. That was the solution to his long wait. He'd spend the extra time at French Hill, and if Louis again had the ague, Angel would stoke the fire, replenish the hot water, and ask for a slice of bread as payment. He turned off the trail and began the steep climb.

As he neared the cluster of buildings, he could see why the Ingots had been late in arriving at the hotel. They had been doing their household chores. Behind each neat little building was a line stretched between two poles. From every line hung a collection of washing, socks, and underdrawers, shirts and pants and towels. The pounded walkways were freshly swept, and even the grass around the flagpole had been cut with a scythe.

For a moment he stood hesitating on the path. Today no smoke issued from the mess hall chimney, and the whole place looked deserted. Then he heard his name called from one of the smaller buildings. Louis Renald was standing in the open doorway.

"Angel! What are you doing here? It is Sunday. Raud does not bake his bread on Sunday."

"I—I came to see if you were all right." Angel was suddenly embarrassed. "You weren't at the hotel with the others. I thought maybe you had the chills."

"My dear friend!" Louis leaped off the single step and rushed over to grasp Angel's arm. "I am touched that you thought of me. But as you see, I am quite well." He threw back his shoulders and pounded with his fists on his chest.

He certainly looked well enough, Angel decided, although a little odd, for his only garment was a towel, which he had knotted about his bare waist. Louis read his thoughts and laughed.

"It is washday," he explained. "Everything else is on the line. Everything except my handsome uniform, and that I must begin saving for my trip."

"You are going away?"

"I am going home." Louis took Angel's arm and began leading him toward the small house. "It will be sooner than I expected. Sooner than any of us expected."

"You mean back to France?"

"To La Belle France," repeated Louis joyfully. "I will have enough gold soon to live comfortably, if I am careful. Not lavishly, you understand. I must not throw it away. That is why I did not go with the others to the hotel. I must start saving, and I am not lucky at lansquenet."

By this time they were inside. There was only one room, with a plank floor, and bunks built into the wall. There were two straight chairs and one small table, but Angel required only a quick glance to tell him there was no food in this cabin. He wished they had gone to the mess hall.

"I didn't expect you would be going home so soon," he said politely. "You never said anything about it before."

"It is sudden," admitted Louis. His tone was guarded, but his eyes glittered with excitement. "I had thought I must remain here longer. A year. Maybe two years of freezing my bones in icy water, of aching joints and fever. But now all is changed. Now it will be soon."

"Are the others going too?" Angel wondered how he could bring up the subject of food.

"No, no," declared Louis scornfully. "They are greedy. They want all they can take. Besides, they do not suffer from the ague as do I."

"I've never had ague, either," Angel told him. "Does it make your stomach ache, the way it does when you're hungry?"

"That and more. You ache everywhere. You wish not to live. It is a bad, a terrible feeling. That is why I am so happy to return home." Louis leaned forward, and his voice sank to a whisper. "I will tell you a secret. You will give me your promise, your solemn vow, not to breathe it to a soul?"

Angel held up his right hand, then touched his heart.

"We have found a new vein," whispered Louis. "A rich vein. It is here on our hill, and we are mining it in secret. Every day we take out three times the gold we did before."

"Why, that's wonderful," cried Angel. "No wonder you can go home sooner than you expected."

"Sh!" warned Louis. "Remember your promise. No one must know."

"I won't tell a soul," promised Angel, this time keeping his own voice low. "And I'm glad for you, Louis. I really am."

The Frenchman stood up.

"Come," he invited. "We will go to the mess hall. We will drink a toast to success, and to our secret."

"Good," agreed Angel, jumping to his feet. "And do you think maybe we might have a little bread and cheese along with the toast?"

He stayed at French Hill until the sun disappeared behind the treetops, then he returned to the hotel.

The gaming room was not so crowded now, for many of the miners had remembered how early they had to be at their claims and had gone home. Angel crossed over to where Brandy was still playing, and because his feet hurt from so much walking, he sat on the floor.

"Aren't you tired?" he asked curiously, when the musician finished the number he was playing.

"Tolerable," agreed Brandy, stretching his shoulders. "But I can sleep all week if I want. That is, I used to could," he corrected himself thoughtfully. "Now, me and you's got to spend the week practicing."

"Practicing? You mean songs?"

"That's right," nodded Brandy. "Didn't the professor tell you?"

"I haven't seen the professor."

"Oh," nodded Brandy, laying his violin on the floor and reaching for the harmonica. "Well, he will, when he gets around to it."

Angel sang twice that evening, and after his second

performance the miners began leaving the tables. Monsieur Leger was disconsolate.

"I thought they would stay longer," he confessed bitterly. "I thought that with entertainment, they would remain."

"So they did," Brandy reminded him dryly, as he slid a wooden case from under his chair and began putting his violin away. "We're closing up a whole hour later than we generally do on Sunday."

"That is so." Monsieur Leger was restored to happiness. "You have done well, boy. Be sure to return next Saturday."

Angel nodded wearily. It was almost midnight, and he was tired. His feet burned, and he wondered how he would be able to drag himself over the trail to Red's cabin.

As he made his way between the empty tables, someone called his name. Joaquin was sitting alone at his deserted monte table.

Slowly Angel made his way across the room. When he looked at his old friend, it was as though he were seeing him through new eyes. This was Murieta, the most celebrated bandit in all California! But he was also the associate of a vicious killer. Angel could make excuses for stealing, but not for murder. He did not see how Joaquin could either.

"I am sorry that I missed you." Joaquin's brown eyes smiled up at him. "Rosita told me you were there, but could not stay. It was only a little after you left that I returned. When I reached Jackson, my old aunt was much improved so I did not remain as long as I expected."

197

"You went to Jackson?" asked Angel curiously. For some reason the name of the town sounded wrong. He didn't think it was the same place Rosita had mentioned that afternoon.

"To Jackson," repeated Joaquin positively. "How did you like my house? Quite different from that cold tent on Loma Linda, eh?"

"It's beautiful," Angel told him honestly. "You must be very rich."

"Not rich," corrected Joaquin, smiling. "But I like nice things around me. And I have been lucky." He began separating the coins and dust on the table into piles.

"Rosita looked well," said Angel. He was having trouble making conversation with his old friend. "And very fine and grand."

"My Rosita is a beautiful woman," declared Joaquin. "It pleased her that you came. We do not forget our friends, and we are happy when they do not forget us. You will come again?"

"I'll come again," agreed Angel, and turned to go. He suddenly felt disturbed and uneasy, and he was afraid that his feelings might show on his face.

Chapter 16

The moment Angel stepped into the kitchen of the Leger Hotel the next day, he knew that something was wrong. The room was filled with the sound of chattering tongues. The employees were gossiping as loudly, and their faces were as long and serious as on the morning Chung Far had been found murdered. He unloaded his bread onto the table, then sought out the cook who spoke the best English.

"What is it?" he demanded. "What's happened?"

"Murieta!" The man's hands waved wildly, and he glanced over his shoulder as though he expected to find the bandit lurking behind the soup pot. "He has struck again. Yesterday. At dawn. Three men were killed, shot dead in the heart. The fourth was shot too, but he did not die. Not yet."

"Where was this? Where did it happen?" Angel shook

his head to clear away the instant recollection of a thin, scarred face and a hawk-beaked nose.

"Close to here. A camp called West Point."

West Point! Angel had heard that name before, and recently. Why, West Point was where Rosita had told him Joaquin had gone to visit his sick aunt!

"Where is West Point?" His voice shook with anxiety.

"North. A little way in the mountains." The arm in the white sleeve waved vaguely. "A small camp. On Sundays the miners come here to our bank sometimes."

Angel told himself he should be ashamed for that moment of doubt. Joaquin said he had gone to Jackson, and he would certainly know where he had been. Rosita was mistaken. Jackson was in the opposite direction from West Point. It was the other Joaquin, the one who killed, who had committed this last crime. Just the same, he felt guilty. He ought to tell someone his suspicions, and soon, before it happened again. It was too much for him to carry alone.

He took his time with the day's deliveries, and it was midafternoon when he started back to Red's cabin. The ascending trail wove in and out of trees and brush, so that long before he reached the cabin he could hear the sound of gunshots. With his mind filled with thoughts of bandits, he began to run. Perhaps the Quins had been attacked! Perhaps the bad Joaquin was dissatisfied with what he had done at West Point and was picking off the outlying cabins on Mok Hill! Angel had no idea how he could help, but he had to get there.

As he came into the open he stopped, the fear dissolved into resentment. It wasn't bandits at all. It was just Rowena showing off with her silver-handled revolver.

She had a new audience, Brandy Wiener, who occupied a stump, while she stood beside him and shot targets on a tree.

She was being more of a braggart than ever, Angel observed, for instead of shooting straight she was doing tricks. She shot over her shoulder, and, from seeing a momentary flash of sunlight, he guessed that she had brought out Mrs. Quin's looking glass and was fixing her target in the reflection, so that she wouldn't have to turn at all. It was the most disgusting performance Angel had ever seen, and his lower lip dropped in a sneer.

Brandy greeted his arrival with an absent-minded nod, then he returned his attention to Rowena.

"Try some more with the mirror," he advised. "You need more practice on that."

"It's hard. I never did it before," objected Rowena, but she turned her back on the tree and focused the target in the mirror.

Angel did not bother to watch. He walked over to Mrs. Quin, who was gathering up dry laundry from the bushes around the clearing.

"Rowena's wasting a lot of good bullets," he reminded her significantly. "I thought they were expensive."

"They are." Mrs. Quin's words snapped with disapproval. "But it's your musician friend's money that's going up in smoke. I let Rowena shoot one bullet to sort of entertain him while he waited for you. After that nothing would do but he must pay for the rest of the bullets I was saving for rabbits and such. And now he's got her shooting crazy ways."

Angel was more resentful than ever. Brandy Wiener

202

had come to see him, to teach him more songs before the next weekend, but now he seemed to have forgotten all about it. He began helping Mrs. Quin collect sun-dried socks and shirts and underwear.

They returned to the cabin just in time to hear Rowena announce that there were only three more bullets.

"Then save them," Brandy ordered quickly. "I want your pa to see this. He's going to be flabbergasted when I point it out. Sometimes a man's so close to the woods, he can't see the trees." Abruptly, he turned his attention to Angel. "Come here, boy," he shouted. "I got to learn you a heap of songs, and we better get started."

Brandy Wiener did not have Mrs. Quin's patience as a teacher. He played through the melody on his har-monica, then repeated the words once and expected Angel to remember both and put them together. Every time Angel forgot, Brandy flew into a rage.

"Use your wits, boy," he shouted. "Use your wits."

"There's at least five verses to that song, and you spoke them off once," objected Mrs. Quin indignantly, as she passed by on her way to the woodpile. "Who could ex-pect him to remember them all?"

"I do, that's who," snapped Brandy. "All right, boy. I'll say them once more, and this time you get them words fixed in your wits."

Angel did his best. Doggedly he went through song after song, but by now the different lyrics had become so mixed up in his mind that he didn't know one from another. It was with relief that he saw Professor Quin's tall figure making its way up the slope.

Brandy saw him, too. That time he didn't even notice when Angel forgot and substituted la, la, la for part of the words. He waited impatiently until the professor was in calling distance.

"Well?" he shouted.

"It is settled." The professor was smiling, a smug smile as though he was very proud of himself. "I told you he would be agreeable. Mr. Ballard is a lonely man, but not from choice. He is merely shy, and requires drawing out. That I have done. He looks forward to a position of public esteem and distinction, and an opportunity to meet with people and receive their applause."

"You trying to tell me that Snuffy's coming too?" Brandy's voice was heavy with misgivings.

"He is coming too," agreed Professor Quin firmly. "It was the only way, but I am sure that it will work out. We shall, of course, obtain for him new and proper raiment. And who knows? Perhaps, with a bath and a few suggestions here and there— At any rate, he will be helpful with the horses."

"I could have handled them," declared Brandy scornfully, but a moment later his mind jumped to another subject. "Look here, Professor. You overlooked a bet. That gal of yours. Do you know she's a deadeye shot?"

"Rowena?" Professor Quin seemed startled. "I suppose she has some prowess with firearms. But I do not see—"

"Then let me tell you." With an impatient jerk of his head, he dismissed Angel, who left as rapidly as possible.

Mrs. Quin was bending over the fireplace crane as Angel entered the hot little cabin. She turned her flushed face to look at him.

"Is your friend staying to supper?"

"He's not my friend," Angel told her, frowning.

"He was being mean to you," said Rowena sympathetically. "He's a funny man. Why did he want me to do all that shooting over my shoulder? It's sort of fun, but it's no way to hunt game. Too risky. Zeb Grant wouldn't stand for it for one minute."

"Your father's calling you, Rowena," said Mrs. Quin wearily. "Mr. Wiener must be ready for you to shoot the last three bullets he made you save. While you're there, ask if he's staying to supper."

Rowena nodded. She took the revolver and her mother's looking glass from the table and went outside.

Angel sat down, his eyes following Mrs. Quin as she went about her supper preparations. The wood box was empty, and it was his job to fill it, but for the moment he was too tired to move. Even his brain was tired. It had been working overtime worrying about the stolen watch, after which it had been compelled to work again memorizing new songs. He knew that Brandy and the professor were involved in some scheme, together with the unpleasant Snuffy Ballard, but he was too exhausted to think about it.

"You mustn't get your feelings hurt by people like Mr. Wiener," said Mrs. Quin after a while. "They're not worth stewing about. I doubt if he memorized the words to all those songs the first time he heard them through, either."

Angel smiled at her weakly. Red was right; Mrs. Quin was a good woman. She was the best person in the whole family. He dragged himself up off the log and outside to fill the wood box.

Mrs. Quin always waited supper for Red Kirk, and it was dusk by the time he returned. As usual, he went straight to the shed, where he changed into dry clothes, and Angel brought him a basin of hot water and soap so he could wash. It was a time Angel looked forward to each day, a few moments when he and Red were alone and could exchange confidences.

"You remember when you said the professor was up to something?" He raised his voice above the splashing and gurgling sounds made by the miner. "And you said it had something to do with Snuffy Ballard?"

Red nodded, groping for the towel.

"Brandy Wiener's mixed up in it now," reported Angel.

"That so?" Red grinned at him. "That's a fine trio, ain't it? Anything else new?"

For a moment Angel considered telling Red about Joaquin. But he knew he couldn't do that. Even Red might not understand the difference between a thief who killed and one who didn't.

"Three miners were shot yesterday at West Point," he said instead. "They think Murieta did it."

Red began to swear.

"That varmint's getting too close for comfort," he declared. "We better get us up a posse and flush him out. It'd be worth a day or two away from the diggings to know a man's dust was safe."

Angel was silent. A posse wouldn't have to look very far to find Murieta's hideout.

"I got a little news too," said Red after a moment. "There's a rumor all up and down the diggings that the Ingots have made a new strike. Rich pay dirt."

"How'd they hear about that?" Angel was startled. Only yesterday Louis had sworn him to secrecy, and

he was sure the other Frenchmen wouldn't want the news made public either.

"Probably turned in more dust than usual at the bank yesterday." Red began gathering up his wet clothes. "Pretty hard to hide a good strike. But some of the boys is mighty riled up. They claim it ain't fair, the

Ingots being furriners, and that something ought to be done. They're working themselves up into a real lather."

"I think they're jealous," decided Angel. "They just don't want somebody else to find more gold than they do."

"You put your finger on it right there," agreed Red sagely. "Of course, they'll give you a heap of excuses. It's American gold and should be for Americans, and all that tommyrot. But it's nothing but plain, downright jealousy. Well, come on. I'm empty clear down to my toes. Let's see what Mrs. Quin's got cooked up for us."

Brandy Wiener stayed to share their supper. It was a silent meal because everyone was too hungry for conversation. But when the big kettle of rabbit stew had been scraped clean, Professor Quin pushed back his plate. Smilingly he looked around the gathering, and his eyes settled upon Red.

"Mr. Kirk, the time has come to thank you for your generous hospitality, and to inform you that we will not infringe much longer on your goodness," he declared in deep, rolling tones.

"You're going away? Back to Oregon, maybe?" Red stared at him in surprise, and Angel heard a funny little catch that was his own breath as it stopped for a moment.

"Not to Oregon," denied the professor, smiling. "No, we shall stay here. It is in the Mother Lode where we expect to find gold, although I admit that we shall make forays to both the northern and the southern mines to do so."

"Thaddeus, I demand to know what you've got up your sleeve." Although Mrs. Quin tried to keep her voice stern, she could not conceal a slight quiver.

"My dear, your husband has conceived the most brilliant idea of his entire career," he told her proudly. "It is the fulfillment of my destiny. It is the reason I was born, although, I must confess, I did not see it before. I propose to embark upon the life of a thespian."

"A thespian? You mean an actor?" she cried in alarm.

"Ah, but I will be more than that," he assured her quickly. "I will also be producer, manager, and businessman. I propose to bring to these entertainment-starved miners the best of the arts. And they are hungry for them. I have proved that to my own satisfaction. Even Mr. Ballard was moved by my scenes from *Romeo and Juliet*. Rivulets ran down his unwashed cheeks while he rocked that infernal cradle of his and listened to their tragic deaths. Likewise, he was moved to laughter at the antics of Shakespeare's several clowns, and I could almost see a kindling of light in his eyes as I repeated King Richard's stirring speeches."

"You mean you're going traveling from camp to camp spouting poetry and such," deduced Red shrewdly. "You figure if Snuffy Ballard liked it, everybody will."

"Exactly," agreed the professor. "But that will not be the end of our entertainment. Our bill will also include Mr. Brandy Wiener, musician extraordinary, virtuoso of the violin and harmonica. It will include Angel Palma, boy soprano, whose flutelike tones will bring a touch of nostalgia to each lonely mining camp. And it will also include Rowena Quin and her unerring re-

209

volver, beautiful young mistress of a deadly weapon."

"Papa!" cried Rowena, beginning to smile broadly.

"I won't have it," cried Mrs. Quin angrily. "I won't have my daughter performing in front of a bunch of tipsy miners. And I won't go traipsing off on any such fool's errand, either."

"My dear, my dear," objected Professor Quin quickly. "Have we not imposed on Mr. Kirk long enough? That is a fact you have been dinning in my ears for many weeks. And truly I cannot, as a gentleman, allow my wife to support me any longer while she washes dirty linen. What other course is then open to us? Besides, this is a splendid opportunity. We will make a fortune."

"It'll take a fortune to get started, too," Red reminded him dryly. "You'll have to have a team and wagon. Likely you'll want costumes—"

"Magnificent ones," agreed the professor promptly.

"And you'll have to pay board along the way, and for printing up posters to advertise your show. It'll take a lot of money."

"All will be taken care of," the professor assured him. "Tomorrow I leave for San Francisco to order the necessary supplies, the costumes, the wagon, the horses, the posters. Whatever we need will be purchased there."

"And where do you think you're going to get the money for all this, Thaddeus? Who'd be fool enough to give it to you?" demanded Mrs. Quin.

"Why, Mr. Ballard." He looked at her in surprise. "I thought you understood. He is a man with great vision, and he is financing everything."

Angel jumped up and ran over to Red. He wound his arms around the miner's biceps and hung on tightly.

"I won't go," he cried. "You can't make me. I'm going to stay right here with Red."

Chapter 17

In his own personal misery, Angel almost forgot the problem of what to do about Joaquin. The week that followed was one of the unhappiest he had ever known. It was almost as bad as those days in San Francisco before he met Pierre. In a way, this was even worse, because that first time he had been numbed by the death of Mamacita. Things had just happened, one after another, so fast he could hardly think. Now all he could do was anticipate, and nothing in his future looked pleasant.

He had been happy here on Mok Hill. He had made friends, especially Red, but there were other friends as well. Soon he would have to leave everyone but the Quins behind, and spend his days with the exacting Brandy Wiener and the smelly Snuffy Ballard.

The night when the professor had told them about his proposed troupe of traveling entertainers and Angel

had declared he wouldn't go, Red had tried to take his part. He had assured the professor that he would be glad to assume responsibility for Angel, that the boy was welcome to remain with him on Mok Hill.

To this the professor would not agree. The authorities in San Francisco had turned Angel over to him. Out of his own pocket he had paid the orphan's expenses. He had given of his valuable time and experience in voice lessons. Now, when the moment had come to realize some return from these investments, he did not intend to step aside. Angel's songs were well received by the miners at the Leger Hotel. He would be a valuable addition to the new company. He must come along.

"There's something to what he says," agreed Red soberly. "You've got to keep your part of the bargain, Angel. It's only honest. But if something should happen, if things don't work out and the company goes ker-plunk, you get onto a stage bound for Mok Hill. Tell the driver I'll pay your fare when he delivers you here."

"Incredible!" Professor Quin had snorted with disbelief. "We shall be a great success. One triumph after another lies before us."

Mrs. Quin had not joined further in the conversation. After her first objections, she had remained quiet, and in the week that followed she grew even more so. Angel observed that the lines of her face grew sharp, the way they had been when he first met her, and her eyes were sometimes red, as though she had not slept well the night before.

Once he asked her opinion of the traveling troupe. "Maybe it'll work," she told him wearily. "Anyway, it's what Thaddeus has set his mind on. It's plain to see that he's not cut out for mining. We'll just have to give it a try."

On Saturday morning, Angel reluctantly gave notice to the little French baker, but Raud was not nearly so upset as he had expected.

"Perhaps it is best," he agreed. "I have heard you sing at the hotel. You are destined for greater things than delivering bread. But I hope," he added anxiously, "that you will continue as long as you can."

"I'll keep on till the professor gets back from San Francisco," promised Angel. He could not help feeling a little letdown. At least, Raud could have said he was sorry to lose his delivery boy.

"What's going on in town?" he asked, abruptly changing the subject. "There must be a hundred miners on the street. Anybody would think it was Sunday, not Saturday."

"I do not know." Raud's voice was anxious. "Nor does Monsieur Leger, although he is usually the first to be told. The men began appearing an hour ago, and they stand in groups that talk, talk, talk. I went outside once, but the talk ceased. They looked at me oddly."

"Has there been another robbery?" Angel felt a lump beginning to form in his chest. He should have told his suspicions about Joaquin to someone. It was just that his mind had been filled with other matters.

"I have not heard of one. And the men are not carrying guns, so it cannot be the Vigilantes. They have only pickaxes and sticks."

"Maybe I can hear something when I go by." Angel

214

gathered up the bread for the hotel and started out the door. "I'll tell you if I do."

Although he passed quite close to several groups of miners, the same thing happened to him as to Raud. The men stopped talking as soon as they saw him coming and stood silently until he was out of earshot. Angel nodded and called out greetings to the men he knew. They answered briefly but did not smile. Everyone's face was serious, and a number looked flushed with anger.

"It's a funny thing," he told Raud when he returned. "Looks like they're working up to something, but I don't know what. It's not all the miners, just some. Red isn't there, or I'd ask him what's going on."

"Whatever it is, I do not like it," declared Raud. He pushed the baskets of bread for the Ingots into Angel's arms. "Go as swiftly as you can. It is not a good day to be on the street."

The mystery of the miners faded from Angel's mind as he traveled the familiar trail out of town. By this time he knew every rise of ground, every turn, every tree and clump of bushes that lined the path. How he hated to leave this. The narrow, sandy streets of San Francisco and those that climbed the cliff to Valparaiso had never been so dear. He passed the long, low, unpainted buildings that housed the Chinese miners, and began the winding climb, between stands of manzanita and jack pine.

He had nearly reached the turnoff to French Hill when he heard the sound. It came from the trail behind, and at first he thought it was a sudden wind in the treetops or a hive of swarming bees. Then he knew it couldn't be either. It was the voice of men, angry men. He had heard just such a threatening rumble from human voices before, and he would never forget it.

"The Hounds!" he cried. Clutching his baskets, he began to run as he had run that night in San Francisco.

By now he could pick out words and sentences.

"Down with them Frenchies!"

"Run them Ingots off! Send 'em packing!"

"American gold for American citizens!"

"Get them furriners off our soil!"

Now he knew. It wasn't the Hounds. It was the miners who had been gathering all morning in the town, the same miners who applauded his songs in the hotel, who toiled over their gold pans and cradles in icy streams from dawn to dusk. They had gone suddenly mad with greed over someone else's good fortune.

There was no longer any need to run. The miners were intent on the Ingots. They would not bother him, not if he stayed out of their path. He carried his baskets to the side of the trail and set them under a scraggly pine.

By this time, the miners had rounded the last turn. Massed in close formation on the trail, there were even more of them than there had seemed in town. Their faces were red and angry, and they brandished pickaxes and stout sticks as they pushed on past the boy, shouting threats and flourishing their improvised weapons as they advanced on French Hill.

Angel felt sick inside. All he could think of was Louis Renald, who had hoped to leave this place before long. What the miners would do to the Frenchmen, he didn't know, but, even though there were no guns in sight, it wouldn't be pleasant. He wished there was something he could do to help, but he could think of nothing. Even if he returned to town to sound the alarm, it would be too late. The other miners, those who had not joined in this expedition, were away on scattered claims. It would be impossible to assemble them before night. As for the townspeople—well, there was only Raud and Monsieur Leger and the people who worked for him, and perhaps a dozen shopkeepers. Then he remembered Mex Town, farther down the trail. Maybe the people there would help.

He scrambled to his feet, but the next minute he began jumping up and down and shouting.

"Joaquin! Joaquin! Hurry!"

Riding toward him on a black horse came a familiar figure. The sun glittered on the silver band of his wide-brimmed hat, and a little wind tugged at the black hair beneath.

"Amigo," called Joaquin as soon as he was close enough to recognize the boy. "My little friend. What are you doing here? Are you on your way to see me?"

"No. I mean, yes. Joaquin, you've got to do something. Ride back for help. Oh, Joaquin, they're going to be killed!"

"Who is going to be killed?" asked Joaquin calmly. He jumped down from the saddle and led Angel from the center of the road into the shadows cast by the manzanita. "Tell me what has happened. You are not hurt?"

"No." Angel shook his head. Then, as rapidly as he could, he told Joaquin about the angry miners who

217

were swarming French Hill. "I'm afraid they're going to kill all the Ingots," he concluded fearfully.

"That I doubt," denied Joaquin. "There will be some broken bones, some bloodied noses. And the Ingots may lose their claims. They may even be run out of town. But killing—no. These miners do not have the stomach for that."

"But that isn't right either," insisted Angel furiously. "They pay their taxes. The claims belong to them. They found them."

Joaquin shrugged.

"When a man cannot protect what he has, he does not deserve to have it."

It wasn't fair. Louis and the other Frenchmen had lived within the law. They had obeyed all the rules. They had worked as hard as anyone to take the gold from the reluctant earth, and now because they had been lucky, others were stealing it from them.

"Red says when a man stakes out a claim, it's his," Angel remembered bitterly. "Nobody can take it."

"They are all fools," said Joaquin promptly. "Only a fool would jump a claim, and only a fool would work one. It is hard work, mining for gold, *amigo*."

Angel stared at him.

"But once it's worked, Joaquin," he said slowly. "Once a man has taken out the gold—"

"Then it is up to him to protect it," repeated Joaquin. "Then, you see, it is work no longer. Then it becomes almost a game to see who becomes the possessor of that gold."

"You are Joaquin Murieta," declared Angel after a moment. "I knew you were."

218

"Yes," agreed Joaquin, smiling. "And I am also your friend. The friends of Murieta do not tell his enemies who he is. And the friends of Murieta have nothing to fear from him. You know that too."

"Do you—have you ever killed anyone, Joaquin?" Angel's voice was almost a whisper.

"I am a bandit, *amigo*. What would you have me do? Sometimes there is no other way." Then he added reassuringly, "But no friend of Murieta's has ever been harmed."

Joaquin—his Joaquin—was a killer, too! He had admitted it. There weren't good bandits, after all, only bad ones.

Angel raised his head and looked into the smiling brown eyes bravely.

"I can't be your friend, Joaquin. Not any longer," he declared. "I can't be friends with a murderer."

"You do not understand," objected Joaquin gently. "When it is your life or theirs, which would you choose? As I have told you, I do not harm my friends. And I do not steal from them."

The orphans in San Francisco had never stolen from their friends, either, only from strangers. Their code had been the same as the bandit's.

"I used to be a thief," admitted Angel slowly. "I stole things. Not big things like gold, but little things. I don't steal any more. Red says it's bad to steal, and he knows. Even though you don't know the people you're stealing from, it's bad. Maybe they need the things you're stealing, like the Ingots need their gold, so they can go home. They've worked hard to get it, and it's

219

not right to steal. A thief is almost as bad as a murderer."

For a moment Joaquin looked angry. Then he smiled.

"You are young, *amigo*. Much too young to understand. And even if you do not wish to be my friend any longer, I will still be yours. For the sake of the friendship you once gave me, will you keep my secret a little longer? Will you give me until tomorrow before you tell anyone who I am?"

"Yes," agreed Angel quickly. He looked at Joaquin, hoping that the other would know he didn't want to tell at all. Perhaps, if he waited until tomorrow to speak, Joaquin and Rosita could get far away. He didn't want to be responsible for their capture, even though Joaquin was a murderer.

"Good," agreed the bandit gaily. He walked over to where his horse nibbled at the drying grass, and the next moment he was in the saddle. "Since I have only until tomorrow, I must change my plans. I will not go on to town today, after all. *Adios, amigo.*"

After Joaquin had ridden back up the trail to Mex Town, Angel sat down on the ground. He had decided that it would be best to wait until the miners left, and then continue on to French Hill. He was a little afraid to go, for he had no idea what he would find, but someone had to.

Now that it was too late, he wished he had not given his promise to keep the secret for another day. By tomorrow, the bandit might kill and rob someone else!

In his mind he went over and over his conversation with Joaquin, and each time he grew more angry with himself. It wasn't enough to say that he couldn't be friends with a murderer. He should have said he despised him. And when Joaquin assured him that his own friends were always safe from harm, Angel should have told him that murderers were also liars and that he didn't believe him for a minute. That was the way the conversation should have gone. Those were the things he should have said. Why was it that he could never think of the right thing to say until it was all over?

For a moment he considered breaking his promise and telling Joaquin's secret today. But he knew he couldn't do that. Red always said that a man who went back on his word wasn't worth the powder it took to blow him up.

Then he thought of still another reason. In his mind he remembered a frightened boy running up a steep hill. Again his ears were filled with sounds he could never forget, the screaming of women and children and the staccato bursts of rifles. Just ahead was a cluster of tents, rising like white ghosts in the starlight, and suddenly a man stepped from one of them.

"In here, *amigo*," he said. "You will be safe here."

Angrily, Angel wiped at his eyes with the back of his hand. Even though Joaquin might have begun his career as an avenger of wrongs, that part of it was now forgotten, and he was all bad. But Angel couldn't forget the man who had been his friend when he needed one. He would keep silent until tomorrow.

He stayed there until late afternoon, and then the miners began drifting back. It was easy to tell that they had been successful. Some looked battered, but their anger was gone. They were smiling and calling triumphant congratulations to one another. When he thought that all of them had gone by, Angel picked up his baskets and started up the hill.

It was very quiet. The occasional shouts and noise which had drifted down to him during the afternoon had ceased. He walked as fast as he could, and he could hear his own heart beating like one of the drums in Jake Plumber's band.

When he reached the top and the little settlement lay before him, he stopped, unable to believe his eyes. Every window in the rows of neat little houses had been shattered. The French flag had been torn from its place, and even the flagpole was broken in half. Many of the doors had been smashed, kicked through by the heavy boots of the miners, and someone had tried to set fire to the mess hall. Luckily, it had been put out, but the white paint was charred and blistered all across the front.

There was no one in sight, so Angel continued on across the square, peering fearfully from side to side. Was everyone dead? Was there not one Ingot left after that mighty battle?

He mounted the single step of the mess hall, and with shaking fingers managed to open the door. Then he heaved a sigh of relief.

There they were! There were the Ingots! And at least some of them were still living, for they sat upright in chairs, with wet cloths on their heads. Others were stretched full length on the floor, but they, too, were alive, for heads raised and eyes turned in his direction.

"Hello," said Angel weakly. "I—I've brought your bread."

He hadn't meant it as a joke, but it must have sounded funny for hysterical laughter rose all around him. Then one of the men limped forward.

"You see, my compatriots!" He spoke with difficulty, because a cut on his lip was swelling fast. "Even after the day's misfortune, life goes on. Here is our daily bread!"

Chapter 18

"Didn't you even guess it was going to happen?" demanded Angel. He addressed the great bulk which was Red's back, preceding him on the dark trail into town. Even after such an eventful day as this had been, there was still his regular singing job at the hotel to be performed.

"I had my suspicions that something was boiling up," admitted Red. "There's a little bunch of soreheads that's been going around sounding folks out about the Ingots. Course, they claimed it didn't have nothing to do with the new strike. They blamed it onto pure patriotism, and the fact that the Ingots flew their own flag on American soil. But most of us knew better."

"Couldn't the rest of you stop them?" For the first time, Angel was a little disappointed in his friend. His voice must have given him away, for Red turned and peered down on him.

"There wasn't too much we could do," he explained, "except wait and bide our time. A good healthy fight to let off steam was what most of us hoped for. And that's what happened. Nobody was hurt so bad they won't get over it. Out and out claim jumping, that's another thing. I wouldn't have stood by for that, and I ain't alone."

"It still wasn't right," insisted Angel stubbornly as they started on again.

Although none of the casualties on French Hill had been fatal, there had been broken bones and gaping cuts. True, some of the miners he had observed descending the hill had similar wounds, but to his mind that didn't even up the score. It was the Ingots' houses that had been wrecked and, because they were the minority, they had received the worst of it. Some of them, like Louis, were so discouraged, and perhaps fearful of future forays, that they said they were going to take what gold they already had and return to France immediately. That wasn't fair, either.

It seemed to Angel that whenever he made a new friend, something happened and he lost him. First Pierre, now Louis, and soon Red. He caught his breath. Losing Red was the worst of all. Since early afternoon he had completely forgotten the professor's scheme which would soon take him away from here.

"Maybe this will be the last Saturday night we'll ever walk to town together," he said mournfully.

"What do you mean by that?"

"Why, next week the professor might come back from San Francisco," explained Angel. "And as soon as he gets here, I'll have to go."

225

"Not a bit of it," objected Red cheerfully. "Way I see it, it'll take the professor and Snuffy at least three weeks before they collect their stuff and get back here. That is, if they're lucky. If they have to send to the East for a wagon, it could take as long as a year."

A year! Why anything could happen in a year! Angel smiled to himself. There was nobody quite so reassuring as Red.

As usual, the hotel was crowded. When they pushed open the doors, hot stale air rushed out to greet them. Angel wrinkled his nose in distaste. In the beginning, he had been too excited to notice the unpleasant odor, but now it struck him full in the face. He'd have to get used to it, he told himself. Professor Quin had already given them warning that their troupe would be performing in rooms like this. As yet, mining camps had no theaters or community halls.

"What are you going to play?" He raised his voice above the noise.

"Thought I'd try faro first," bellowed Red, giving him an affectionate whack on the back. "You sing pretty now. I'll be listening."

His wide shoulders disappeared into the crowd, and Angel began inching his way slowly forward. He knew that he should report immediately to Brandy Wiener, but he delayed that moment as long as he dared.

He had come to dislike the little musician, who now arrived at the cabin every afternoon to take over the singing lessons. There was no pleasing him, and his sharp criticism had a sting about it. Rowena didn't like him either, for Brandy kept her practicing shots with the looking glass all the long hours that Angel was trying to memorize new songs.

"I hate him," she said frankly. "It's no fun to shoot any more. He never says I did well, only that I have to do better."

For the first time, Angel felt a bond of sympathy between himself and Rowena.

As he fought his way through the barricade of red shirts and pieced-out garments of the miners, he could hear a snatch of melody being played on a harmonica. He made a face in the direction of the sound, wishing that Brandy Wiener would fall down and break a leg. Then he couldn't walk to the cabin and bother him and Rowena any more.

It was habit that drew Angel toward the monte tables. On Saturday and Sunday, he always came this way, hoping that Joaquin would look up from his cards to smile. Now he remembered that Joaquin would never be here again. Angel had promised to keep silent only until tomorrow, and his former friend had ridden back to Mex Town, probably to gather up Rosita and make his escape. It made him feel sad to realize that he might never again see the young Mexican whom he had idolized for so long.

As he came within view of the third table, he stopped short in surprise. Joaquin was there, dealing as usual. The slim brown fingers fairly flew as the cards dropped before each player.

Joaquin, Joaquin! thought Angel helplessly. Why don't you run? Do you think I didn't mean it? He stared hard at the dealer, willing him to look up, but Joaquin was too intent. Tonight, he had discarded his fine velvet garments. He wore a soft leather jacket, dyed black, and his shirt was black too, but made of silk. The effect was very somber, like a shadow, or a dark cloud, or as though he were in mourning.

Angel stood there for some minutes, but when Joaquin did not look up, he reluctantly made his way to the other end of the room. He couldn't stall any longer.

Brandy's unsmiling eyes did not bother to acknowledge Angel's arrival. He finished the number he was playing, then slipped the harmonica into his pocket.

"We'll try one of the new ones," he declared. "See that you keep your wits, and don't forget any of the words."

Angel's heart sank. There had been so many new songs in the past week. He wished Brandy would start off with one of the old ones.

Before he had finished the first verse, the room grew quiet. The miners laid down their hands and leaned back in their chairs to listen. Their smiling faces gave Angel the help he needed and the words came to him, but he made one bad mistake in the tune. There was nothing to do but ignore it and continue on to the end.

As the shower of money fell around them, Brandy spoke from the corner of his mouth.

"You fool. That was a high note. You did it right every other verse. How come you hit it sour?"

Angel shook his head. He had intended to sing the right note, but his voice had played a trick on him. It had come out low and off key. He couldn't explain it.

Requests followed, one right after another. Tonight,

thanks to Brandy's tutorage, Angel was able to sing most of them. At the end of ten minutes, Monsieur Leger stepped forward to announce that the first performance was at an end. There would be another at midnight.

Angel had two hours to wait, and because he didn't want to spend them in Brandy's company, he went outside. The air was crisp, and after the heat of the room it felt chilly. He sat down, resting his back against the building, with his legs stretched out across the narrow boardwalk.

It was very dark, a night without a moon, when even the stars seemed pale, but after he had been there awhile they gave enough light to see. Not that there was much to look at, he decided. Except for the hotel and the saloons down the street, the buildings were in darkness. Occasionally, a disgruntled miner would throw back the doors, letting out a flood of warmth and light and smell, and after a time he would disappear into the shadows.

He thought about Joaquin, calmly dealing cards at the table inside. He thought about the Ingots, nursing their wounds on French Hill. Tonight the lansquenet table stood vacant. It might be some time before those who were too stubborn to give up would fill those chairs again. It had been a long, eventful day, and he would be glad when it was over.

The noises from the hotel rushed out from the top and bottom of the swinging doors into the street, but above them he was now conscious of another sound. It was the pounding hoofs of horses. They grew louder by the second, and Angel strained his eyes, peering through the darkness. Another minute, and a rider, leading a second horse, rounded the corner by Raud's bakery. He was followed by two others, and behind them, riding in pairs, galloped even more.

Angel blinked. He had not known there were so many horses on Mok Hill. The livery stable kept teams and a few riding horses for rent, but when a miner did not travel on foot or stage, he usually depended on a mule. Why, there were at least forty horses, maybe more, in this group! And they did not come from the outside. They used the road that led to French Hill and to Mex Town on beyond, which meant they had been here all along.

The first rider pulled up his mount at the hotel, directly in front of the spot where Angel was sitting, and the others did the same. They were quiet. No one said a word, and even the horses seemed trained to silence, for there was none of the usual nickering and snorting. Angel had to strain to see, for all of the riders were dressed in dark colors that faded into the shadows. Only their faces were pale blurs in the starlight.

Half of them dismounted, and he thought he could see them pass reins to those who remained in the saddles. Then his eyes caught something else, a silver gleam, and he grew cold and shrank back against the wall. They carried guns.

Hastily, he drew his legs up, hoping they would pass him by unnoticed. He was disappointed. A long arm reached down, and hard fingers closed about his shoulder. A moment later, he was jerked to his feet.

"See what I have found. A little spy. Maybe I should

230

cut his throat." The whispered words were in Spanish, and Angel understood them very well.

"You put me down," he cried loudly. "You leave me alone."

Instead, the man laughed and lifted him higher, bringing their heads close together. For a horrified second, Angel stared into that well-remembered face which had become a nightmare to him. There was the beaked nose, the scar running down one cheek, the hard, cruel eyes and mouth.

"Put him down, Joaquin!" One of the riders called from horseback. It was a woman's voice, but filled with authority. "Put him down and get on with your job."

Deliberately, the bandit's fingers opened, allowing Angel to drop heavily to the walk. As he fell, the boy stared upward at the opened hand that had held him so cruelly. There was a space between two of the fingers; one was missing.

Through his mind flooded remembrance of an almost-forgotten conversation. It was at the beginning of their journey, when the stagecoach had stopped at Shingle Springs.

"That Three-Finger Jack feller don't care about how empty a pocket is," one of the miners had warned. "He just kills for the fun of it. They say he's worse than Murieta, for all he's only second in command."

How stupid he had been, Angel told himself. Even though the two Joaquins operated separately, the robberies were all planned by one man—by his former friend. There was going to be another robbery now, and if Angel had not been so tender-hearted, it would

not have happened. Why had he promised to keep silent until the next day? Why?

By this time the riders had pushed open the swinging doors and were inside the hotel. There was the sound of a single gunshot, followed by a moment of startled silence, after which a man's voice began calling out orders.

Angel stayed where he was, flat on the boards. He was too frightened to move. Then he remembered the woman's voice that had come out of the darkness, and he called to her.

"Rosita."

"Angel?" She answered immediately. "Is that you? I could not see. The darkness—"

"Rosita, don't let Joaquin do these things," he pleaded. "It's not right. Make him go away to Mexico, where he'll be safe. He's got enough now. He doesn't need to steal any more. And don't let him take Three-Finger Jack with him. He's a bad man, Rosita. He kills because he likes to."

"There is no need to hide in Mexico," denied Rosita firmly. "My Joaquin is clever, too clever to be caught. And as for Joaquin Valenquela—the one the gringos call Three-Finger Jack—he has his uses, although, as you say, he does kill needlessly. My Joaquin has told him so many times. But you do not need to fear him, Angel," she added. "Joaquin is your friend, and his friends are sacred."

"But—"

"Get back now." Again her tone grew firm with authority. "Close against the building. It will be over soon. You must be out of the way."

Even as she spoke, the men began backing through the doors, swinging them wide with the weight of their bodies. In his right hand each man held a gun, in his left a cloth bag, which sagged heavily.

The last one through wore a coat of black leather and a dark silk shirt. He was smiling. As the doors swung shut behind him, he turned. With one leap he was in the road. Another leap and he was in the saddle.

The first men through the door were already galloping away into the night, down the rough dirt road that led off the hill. Shortly they would reach the crossroads, and then it would be anyone's guess which turn they would take.

By now the noise had resumed inside the hotel. Angry miners, silenced at the sight of pointing gun muzzles, had recovered enough to begin shouting threats of retribution. Only Angel heard the voice which floated back from the last departing rider.

"*Yo soy* Joaquin. I am Joaquin, the avenger. Remember me, *amigo*."

Chapter 19

Since Murieta's men had circulated among the tables, relieving the customers of all their gold, the games necessarily came to an end. A group of angry men surged past Angel, who still leaned weakly against the wall, and rushed down the street toward the livery stable. There they commandeered all the horses, and, a few minutes later, he saw them pass again, this time mounted and in hot pursuit.

It wouldn't do any good. Even Angel knew that. Joaquin had a head start and better horses. By this time the bandits would have reached the crossroads. In the pale starlight, even the most skillful tracker would have trouble tracing their route. They could have headed west through Jackson, or east to San Andreas and Angel's Camp. Or they might have used the rough trail through Valley Springs, which would eventually bring them to

Tuleburgh. Probably the pursuers knew it too, but it made them feel better to be doing something.

Angel stood where he was, huddled against the building. After a long time, Red pushed back the double doors and stepped out into the street. His blue eyes squinted from left to right, trying to penetrate the blackness.

"Angel!" he bellowed. "Angel! You out here?"

"Yes," said Angel. His voice was very small.

Red walked over, and his big hand closed gently, protectingly about the boy's shoulder.

"Now this is right smart of you, boy, to get out of that bedlam inside. Leger's closing up for the night. Might as well head for home. You won't have to sing no more."

Angel nodded, and fell into step beside the big miner. He found that his weak legs would carry him after all.

"Joaquin is the famous bandit," he said.

"That's right," agreed Red. "He's a man with two sides to him, Joaquin is. Kind of hurt when he let you see the other one tonight, didn't it?"

"Yes," agreed Angel.

He still remembered that night on Telegraph Hill when Joaquin and Rosita had taken him into their tent. They had been kind to him here too. There had been the gift of the expensive revolver to Rowena. And Rosita had said that their house was his, and that Joaquin's friends were sacred and would come to no harm. Angel couldn't hate them, not even when he knew what they were.

"I didn't see you while it was going on," said Red

sociably. "I stood up and looked for you, too, till one of them threatened to put a hole in me unless I sat down."

"I was outside when they rode up. I wanted some fresh air. There were a lot of them, women too, all on horses. They talked to me." He shivered at the memory of Joaquin Valenquela's cruel face. "I found out about Joaquin this afternoon. I was going to tell you tomorrow. I promised I'd give him until then. But if I'd told you right away, this wouldn't have happened," he added sorrowfully.

"Sometimes it's hard knowing the right thing to do," agreed Red. "The main thing is we're rid of him in these parts, and nobody got hurt tonight except in his poke. Someday they'll catch up with him though. You know that, don't you?"

"I know," agreed Angel. But he was glad that he himself hadn't been the cause of it.

"I had a ringside seat to the whole thing." Red chuckled at the remembrance. "Faro wasn't my game tonight, and I'd just moved over to Joaquin's table when it happened. Swede Peterson was there, and for some reason the talk drifted to Murieta. That was before his band of ruffians appeared, you understand."

Angel nodded.

"Well, Swede laid down his poke and says there was about five hundred in dust in it, and he was willing to bet anybody there that he'd blast Murieta the first time he laid eyes on him, on account of he had a special sense that let him smell out bandits. And at that very moment, the others busted through the doors and fired that shot in the air. Swede's mouth just plumb fell off its hinges when Joaquin reached across the table to pick up the poke. 'I'll take that bet,' he says, cool as you please."

Red laughed uproariously, and Angel managed a weak smile. He knew that Red was trying to be diverting because it hurt to lose a friend.

"Did you lose very much tonight?" he asked.

"Not much," admitted Red blithely. "Mrs. Quin saw to that. She made me leave most of it behind to take to the bank tomorrow."

All week the residents of Mok Hill talked of nothing but the revelation that Joaquin Murieta had been living in their midst. They were not alone. The people of the surrounding towns and camps talked about it too, and finally a committee was formed to make a formal protest at the state capital.

Red claimed it was like locking the barn door after the horse was stolen, for Joaquin and his men had moved on permanently. A scrutiny of Mex Town yielded nothing but a cluster of patched adobes and a handful of ignorant peons, mainly women and children. There were no reports of a richly furnished house, so Angel concluded that Rosita had hidden most of her possessions and taken the rest along.

Close by, in a secluded spot, a fine, large corral was found. It would have held many horses, and there was hay scattered about and even a few oats. It was the only remaining evidence that the most famous bandit in all of California had once headquartered there.

By the end of the week, the excitement had died down, and life was once more back to normal.

With the professor still in San Francisco, there were

no singing lessons in the morning, and Angel spent those hours helping Red. He took turns rocking the cradle and shoveling dirt. Almost before he knew it, the sun was overhead and it was time to leave for the bakery. When he returned, Brandy Wiener was waiting at the cabin to teach him the words to new songs. Rowena would already be practicing with her revolver, and the sharp sputter of her gunfire would continue all the time he was singing.

"Seems to me we used to do that one in a different key," observed Brandy one day. "You got a cold, boy?"

"No," denied Angel shortly. He refused to confess that it was becoming a strain to reach some of the high notes he had once taken so easily. And sometimes the notes came out sour. He didn't need Brandy's glare to tell him. He could hear it himself.

"Maybe I been working you a mite too hard," decided Brandy reluctantly. "Even a fiddlestring breaks after so long. You rest awhile. I'll go give the girl a few pointers with her shooting."

After that Brandy gave him frequent rest periods, and much to Rowena's disgust, spent more time overseeing her practice. She was getting very good at trick shooting. Even Angel admitted it. The newest stunt consisted of shooting between her legs. She had to pin up her skirts to do it, and Angel was surprised that her mother permitted it. Mrs. Quin, however, didn't pay much attention to what was going on. She went about her daily chores as though her mind were occupied with other matters.

One day when Angel arrived at the bakery, he found the room crowded with excited, chattering Ingots, all speaking French, and dressed in their Sunday uniforms of blue and white.

During the weeks since the battle on the hill, they had kept to themselves, even avoiding the lansquenet tables at the hotel. Those who were able had returned to their claims, while the others waited for broken bones to mend. Now they were here in full force.

"Angel!" Louis Renald shouted from across the room and began elbowing his way through the crowd. "I am glad you came before the stage arrived. I would not have liked to leave without saying goodbye."

"Are you going back to France?" Angel had to yell to make himself heard.

Louis nodded, smiling. He slipped his arm through Angel's and drew him outside where they could talk more quietly.

"I didn't know you were all leaving," said Angel.

"Not all. Perhaps half. The others insist on staying here, but they are foolish," declared Louis scornfully. "What happened once could happen again. It is safer to take what we have and go. The stage has been sent for. Soon we will be away from here forever."

"I'm sorry. I'll miss you, Louis." As soon as he said the words, Angel looked startled. His voice had come out wrong. It had started as usual, but the last two words had dropped a full octave.

Louis laughed gaily.

"You are becoming a man," he observed. "Your voice is changing. If I ever see you again, you will not be a soprano. You will be a bass."

So that was the explanation for the recent sour notes

and Angel's inability to reach the high ones! It had never happened before when he was talking.

"How long does it take?" he asked curiously.

Louis shrugged. He could not remember. Besides, it was of no importance. It happened to every boy. The important thing was that he, Louis Renald, was shaking the dust of Mokelumne Hill from his feet forever.

Angel saw his friend off on the stage, and listened carefully to his own voice every time he spoke. It did not break again that afternoon, but as soon as he returned to the cabin, he told Brandy Wiener. It seemed only fair.

"You'll have to think up a better excuse than that to get out of work," scoffed Brandy. "Keep your wits about you now. This song's got a lot of verses, and I'm only going to say them through once."

During his rest period, Angel tried to tell Mrs. Quin. She was bending over the fire, pulling out a heavy flatiron that had been heating in the coals.

"Mrs. Quin, I think my voice is changing."

"I doubt it." She wiped ashes from the iron with a rag. "You're only ten. That's too early."

"I lied," he admitted bravely. "I'm really twelve."

She looked at him with sadly sympathetic eyes.

"You can't get out of it by fibbing, Angel. Thaddeus has made up his mind, and there's no changing him. You'll have to go. We'll all have to go."

Only Red believed him. When Angel reported the incident later that evening, the miner nodded solemnly.

"Happens to all of us," he said. "Sometimes it's a humiliating time, too. I can remember when I changed from a soprano to bass. Never did know how it was going to come out when I opened my mouth."

"That's the way it was with me this afternoon," remembered Angel. "But it hasn't happened again."

"Might not happen for quite a spell," Red told him. "As I recollect, it's sort of like cutting a tooth. Works awhile, then stops. Then it starts working again. But when it really gets going, when you're smack in the middle, then you can never trust it to stay steady."

"How long will that be?" asked Angel hopefully. "The professor won't want me if my voice is changing."

"By the time he gets back, you should be full into it," promised Red. "One minute you'll sound like some angel, and the next word will come out squawking like a jay bird."

After that, Angel listened to himself carefully whenever he spoke, hoping that his voice would break in the middle of a sentence. Sometimes it would go on for a day or two in the usual tones, but occasionally it would play tricks on him. The sad part was that it never happened when he was with Brandy or Mrs. Quin. Rowena heard it once, but she insisted that he was doing it on purpose, and he couldn't convince her otherwise.

The sour notes appeared more frequently in his songs, but the miners didn't care. Brandy lowered the key on all the music and grumbled a lot about a human voice not being so dependable as a jew's-harp.

One evening as they were sitting down to supper, there was a loud pounding at the door. Darkness came earlier these days, and there was a chill in the air that promised winter was on its way.

242

Rowena got up to answer the knock. For a moment she stood staring into the darkness, then she gave a little squeal.

"Papa!"

Professor Quin stepped into the room and for a moment he stood there, allowing everyone to admire his magnificence. He wore all new clothing, a tall, shining hat and a voluminous fur-collared cape over a black suit with a swallow-tailed jacket. Across a scarlet vest was suspended a heavy gold watch chain, and although his shoes were now dusty from the trail, they had once gleamed as brightly as his glossy hat.

"As you perceive, we return victorious from our pilgrimage," declared the professor grandly. With a swoop of his arm, he drew forward his companion.

This was a smaller figure, but equally resplendent. Instead of a silk hat, the man wore a bowler, and his choice had been a long broadcloth coat instead of a cape. Where it parted, there was a glimpse of yellow vest and bright blue necktie. He stood without speaking, regarding them with shy self-consciousness.

"Snuffy?" asked Red after a moment. "Snuffy, is that you?"

"Not Snuffy. Horace," corrected the professor, frowning. "Horace T. Ballard, financier of the entertainment world. Proprietor of Professor Quin's Traveling Company Par Excellence." He crossed the room and bent over his wife's cheek. "How are you, Almira?"

"I'm fine, Thaddeus," she said weakly.

"And Rowena, my dear, how goes it with the revolver practice?"

"Fine, Papa. I've got three new tricks to show you."

"And Mr. Kirk? Our generous host." The professor was making the rounds, greeting everyone in turn.

"Tolerable," admitted Red, who could not take his eyes from the new Snuffy Ballard.

"And Angel? Have you mastered many new songs? Do you practice every day?"

"Yes, sir. I practice every day," said Angel clearly. Then his voice gave way, and he added in a quavering baritone, "I learned a lot of new songs."

Chapter 20

"We've got to save a seat for Mrs. Quin," Angel reminded Red as they climbed the trail from the diggings to the cabin. "She wants to see the show from out front, but she doesn't want to sit by herself."

"We'll save it," Red grinned down reassuringly. "Leger's got three seats marked off in the front row for you and me and Mrs. Quin. Nobody else can sit in them."

"And we'd better hurry," added Angel. "We don't want to be late."

He had never seen a show. Even the word sounded a little vague, but he knew it was going to be exciting.

Before the new wagon, which bore on its painted side the information that it transported "Professor Quin's Traveling Company Par Excellence, Horace T. Ballard, Prop.," rolled out of town tomorrow, the company was giving a performance at Monsieur Leger's hotel. It was midweek, but the posters had been up on the buildings for several days, and everyone in Mokelumne Hill planned to attend.

Angel had been watching the sun all day, afraid they might miss the opening number. He was helping Red full time now, for Raud had decided to discontinue delivering bread to his customers. Monsieur Leger had arranged to send a cook's helper for his supply and only a handful of stubborn Ingots remained on the hill. Regular miners, declared the baker, could just wear out their own shoe leather to pick up their bread. Brandy was leaving the hotel, so there would be no accompanist, even if Angel could sing. He knew that he mustn't do that. Professor Quin had made it very clear that a boy whose voice was changing must not sing a note until it was all over. Something dreadful would happen to it if he did.

"Of course, you understand that this makes it impossible for you to accompany us," he explained frankly. "It would not be fair to Horace. Everyone must perform some function in our little company, and you would be dead weight."

"He might as well stay with me then," said Red, winking at Angel. "I'll see to it that he performs some function. It'll be lonesome around here with all of you gone. He'll be company."

It was what Angel wanted, but he was a little disappointed that he'd never be able to wear the glittering gold suit the professor had brought back for him. It wouldn't do him any good around here, though, and Mrs. Quin said she could make it over for Rowena. It would be appropriate for the trick where she shot the revolver between her legs.

Angel and Red washed in tepid water, for they had forgotten to bank the fire and it had gone out with no one to tend it. After it was rebuilt, they spread their sodden garments to dry, then got their own supper, beans and bread and warmed-up coffee.

"Remember when Mrs. Quin used to have it ready for us?" asked Angel, chewing on a crust. "And sometimes there was rabbit stew, if Rowena'd been lucky?"

"Hush, boy," chided Red. "The Quins have only been gone and living at the hotel a week. It'll get worse. Lots worse. Unless you want to change your mind about staying?"

"No," declared Angel. "I don't want to change my mind." His voice went up and down in the middle of the sentence, and they exchanged amused grins. It wasn't so bad having your voice play tricks on you if you had someone like Red to share the joke.

A fine rain was falling as they traveled the trail into town, and Angel pulled his coat about his neck. It was a new coat that Red had bought him, and there were new shoes on his feet, too.

"Maybe if it gets too lonesome for us this winter," said Red speculatively, "we might take us a trip down to Frisco and see us some sights. I got a little bit put away to pay for it. How's that strike you?"

"To San Francisco?" Angel's excited smile was erased by a look of apprehension. "I don't know, Red. That Sam Brannan—he might catch me and put me in his asylum."

"He couldn't do that," denied Red staunchly. "You got folks now. Me. But we might look in on that friend of yours that you're always talking about. Not that I ain't sure he's not perfectly all right, you understand."

"Pierre," nodded Angel eagerly.

It would be good to see Pierre again. And if he wasn't happy, if he was being mistreated, Angel knew that Red would do something about it. Maybe he'd even bring Pierre here to live with them. Of course, if such a thing should happen he would have to take his old friend aside and explain a few things. Pierre would have to agree to a lot of changes. He couldn't steal, and he'd have to keep his word, once it was given. He couldn't admire people like bandits, not even if they were famous. And he'd have to do his share of the work, because it wasn't fair to eat Red's food and accept the clothes his money paid for without doing something in return. But Angel was sure he could handle Pierre. He always had.

The street was almost as crowded as though it were Saturday night, but there was a difference in tonight's crowd. The townspeople, who always gathered below the flagpole on Sunday, were now collecting for the performance. It seemed strange to see ladies in bonnets and shawls disappear through the swinging doors of the gaming rooms. Of course, the majority of spectators were miners.

Snuffy Ballard, splendid in bowler hat and broadcloth coat, took tickets. He was too overcome to talk to anyone, but he did manage an embarrassed grin when Red clapped him on the shoulders. Angel sniffed as he passed by. Snuffy's old scent had been replaced by one of strong toilet water. It made him think of the fandango girls.

Monsieur Leger had set up rows of benches across the room, and Red proudly led the way to the very first one. It faced an open area, marked off by a rope. On the floor beneath the rope were a dozen oil lamps that flooded this portion of the room with light.

"Well, now," declared Red, settling himself and motioning Angel to sit beside him. "This is real nice. Don't have to look through somebody's head. They can look through ours."

The benches quickly filled with spectators, and when there were no more seats people stood in the back. For a few minutes it was enough for the audience to visit with their friends, but before long they began to grow impatient. Someone whistled, a shrill, piercing blast, and then others began to clap their hands and stamp their feet. They had paid to see a show, and they wanted it to begin.

The door next to the spot where Brandy used to keep his chair opened, and Mrs. Quin stepped through. The shouting and clapping grew louder, and her cheeks flushed scarlet as she ducked under the rope and hurried to sit down in the empty space next to Red.

"My, that's mortifying," she whispered. "If I'd known, I'd have come in the front way."

"It's just that you look so pretty, ma'am," said Red gallantly. "They figured you was part of the show."

"Gracious, no," objected Mrs. Quin, smoothing the skirt of the new satin dress her husband had brought her from San Francisco.

Then Professor Quin stepped through the door and held up his hand for silence.

"We open our performance with a medley of familiar

249

airs performed by that virtuoso of violin and harmonica, Mr. Brandy Wiener," he announced.

When Brandy stepped through the door, his appearance was greeted with loud whistles. Angel knew it was because he was no longer dressed in the baggy pantaloons and faded shirt. Instead he wore a purple satin suit with lapels of yellow velvet.

"The trouble I had taking that suit in to fit that man you'd never believe," whispered Mrs. Quin. "Between him and Rowena, I've not had a thimble off my finger all week."

Brandy's numbers were well received, since he specialized in old favorites. Although the miners had heard him play before, they listened tolerantly, realizing that his performance was new to many of the townspeople. He switched from harmonica to violin and back again, but when he began to sense a restlessness among his listeners he bowed himself through the door.

Rowena was next. She wore a blue silk dress trimmed with lace, and her hair hung in long, corkscrew curls instead of pigtails. People gasped and ah-ed as shot after shot found the center of a painted target. She fired with her arm straight ahead and also over each shoulder, and hit whirling disks that the professor tossed into the air. Then she sighted through the mirror, and again she hit the center of the target.

After that, Brandy played a brief interlude while Rowena disappeared to change into the glittering gold suit, and when she returned she did the trick shot between her legs. All over the room people were cheering and exclaiming over her skill, and Angel cheered too. Rowena was good with a gun. Maybe she did a lot of bragging, but she had a right to.

The last act was Professor Quin, who recited poetry. The deep voice thundered in certain passages, then grew calm and soothing. Sometimes it was like a clanging bell, and sometimes it had the gentleness of a light breeze. Angel wasn't always able to follow the meaning of the words, but it was enough to hear that magic voice. He was surprised to feel little goose pimples running up and down his arm.

The room was very quiet all the time the professor was speaking, and when he finally stopped and bowed the applause was deafening.

Mrs. Quin wiped her eyes.

"Maybe he's found it this time," she said prayerfully. "Maybe this time it's right."

"Ma'am, I think it is," Red told her honestly.

Monsieur Leger came bustling to the front of the room.

"Ladies and gentlemen, this concludes the performance," he announced. "But you are welcome to remain and enjoy yourselves. The bar will now open."

With disdainful sniffs, the ladies in the audience arose and started for the door. Most of the miners left too. Morning came very early.

As he and Red mingled with the crowd, Angel listened carefully to what people were saying. Their conversations all seemed to be about the performance, and everyone agreed that it had been a great success. Angel hoped the other mining camps would be as enthusiastic as Mok Hill. He wanted the Quins to be happy. They had done a lot for him. He wouldn't even be here if it hadn't been for them. His whole life would have been different.

"You know," said Red, as they walked along in the darkness, "it's early, but I think I smell snow. What do you say we lay us in a big. log? If we have to hole up, might as well spend the time building a Long Tom. It goes best with three people working it, but the way you're coming on maybe we could manage it between the two of us come next spring. How's that strike you, partner?"

"Fine." Angel smiled happily. "It sounds fine, partner."

Then they both laughed uproariously, because his voice broke, and the word "partner" came out a high squeak.

AUTHOR'S NOTE

From the years 1851 to 1853, the name of Joaquin Murieta was probably the most famous in all California. The Mexicans looked upon him as their hero, one who would avenge the loss of their land and gold to the United States. To the miners he was someone to be feared, and newspapers warned people not to travel in groups of less than six, lest they meet with the most celebrated of all bandits, Joaquin Murieta.

Today, over a hundred years later, his name is not forgotten. As one travels through ghost towns and former mining camps, he will notice that almost every one bears a plaque proudly stating "Joaquin Murieta was here." The gold fields cover many square miles, and between running off cattle, stealing horses, robbing saloons and stores, and robbing travelers, one might think he had spent every waking moment on horseback to cover so much territory.

As a matter of fact, there were five *banditti* leaders, all named Joaquin: Murieta, Carillo, Botilleras, Ocomoreña and Valenquela. The last was Three-Finger Jack, Murieta's lieutenant. Whether the others headed separate bands or all belonged to one, no one knows. But their first name, which was usually announced at the time of a robbery, accounted for the fact that Joaquin could simultaneously commit crimes two hundred miles apart.

In 1853, when Murieta was only twenty-three years old, he was shot from his horse near Cantua Canyon by a posse that had been sent out to capture him. Valenquela was killed in the same battle.

To prove that they had the right men, Murieta's head and Three-Finger Jack's hand were brought back to San Francisco, preserved in alcohol. There they were exhibited in the Market Street Museum until they were destroyed in the Great Fire of 1906.

ABOUT THE AUTHOR

The mother of two daughters, author Evelyn Sibley Lampman is a graduate of Oregon State College and was Educational Director of the Portland, Oregon, NBC radio station for a number of years. Several of her radio scripts have won national awards, and her stories have appeared in many popular magazines.

Mrs. Lampman's first book for young people was published in 1948, and since then she has written many books for children—demonstrating her amazing versatility by writing fantasy, historical fiction, and contemporary fiction with equal skill and success.